A MISSING CONNECTION
A Movie Magic Novella

DANI MCLEAN

A MISSING CONNECTION

Book 3 of The Movie Magic Novella series

Copyright © 2023 by Dani McLean

First edition: March 2023

www.danimclean.com

Cover Design by Ink & Laurel

Edited by Beth Lawson at VB Edits

Author photo by Rachael Munro Photography

Also by Dani McLean

The Movie Magic Novella Series:

Midnight, Repeated

Not My Love Story

A Missing Connection

It Has To Be You - Out May 2023

The Forces of Love - Out July 2023

***

The Cocktail Series:

Love & Rum

Sex & Sours

Risks & Whiskey

For you.
Always remember,
Bravery comes in many forms.
Don't be afraid to be yourself.

Authors Note

The Movie Magic Novella series takes place in the fictional location of Chance city.

Chance is a place where anything can (and frequently does) happen. Characters don't always treat these situations as common place, nor do they find them overwhelmingly strange.

Like your favourite movie rom-coms, the magic and wonder of these stories are never explained. Believe anything you want, as long as it makes you happy.

It is a world of wonder, where anything is possible.

Like a fairytale.

Or a beautiful love story.

Chapter One

As it turned out, thirty-three years had *not* been long enough to prepare for this moment.

CLASSIFIED: CEO Succession Announcement

In summation of today's meeting, current COO Beau Aaron Forrester will succeed his father, long-standing CEO Jonathon Patrick Louis Forrester.

Beau rolled his eyes. Of course JP needed the full length of his name listed.

Effective April 29th. The official announcement will be made to company employees via internal communications and to attending press at the annual Gala Benefit that evening. Prior to this date, this information is HIGHLY CLASSIFIED and must be kept to C-Suite ONLY.

I expect full support of Beau's transition over the next eight weeks.

He closed the email on his phone, letting the room go dark.

No turning back now.

Beau sagged in the chair, the leather groaning with a familiarity he hadn't prepared himself for as he looked around Keaton's empty office. Gone were the photo frames that had littered the desk, the Ivy League degree on the wall, and the toy basketball hoop. Blank surfaces and the strong smell of citrus cleaner were all that was left.

Only the half-dead Ficus in the corner reminded Beau that this had been his best friend's office for four years.

At least everyone had gone home for the night. He'd be hard pressed to explain why the COO was fighting off tears in an empty office on the twenty-fourth floor.

Beau didn't blame Keaton for leaving.

If he'd had a choice, he wouldn't be here either, but his father was the CEO, and Beau's last name was on the building. His wishes had never factored in.

Having Keaton around had softened the blow. One friendly face, a reminder that Beau was more than his bank account or his father's expectations.

Now he was alone, on the cusp of inheriting a kingdom he neither wanted nor felt remotely prepared for.

As sole heir to the Forrester conglomerate empire, he had no choice. There had been no other future for him. No fork in the road. No alternative action. Only this, from the day he was born.

He turned to face the floor-to-ceiling window beside him. The world outside was dark, the city blanketed by nightfall. Only a sparse few lights dotted the neighboring high-rise.

They were sister buildings, separated by a short distance, mirroring each other. Beau scanned the sea of empty offices and hallways.

Empty, except for one.

Directly across from him was a riot of color and life. Posters and papers flooded the office walls, a whiteboard was covered in scribbles, a tall bookcase heaved with hardbacks and frames. Even the desk hadn't been spared. Multiple cups adorned the surface among the array of pads and paperwork.

It was chaos.

Beau's office — his official one on the top floor — was the complete opposite, sterile and cold. Everything JP wanted him to be.

Commandeering Keaton's office gave him an escape. A means to keep a sliver of himself within this concrete cage.

Movement caught his attention, and Beau's breath caught as a rush of auburn hair and a fluttering floral dress floated into the office he'd been watching. The woman cupped a mug between her hands and did a double take when she saw the cups already littering the desk. He covered his growing smile under one hand as the cup hoarder spent a few minutes searching for a free space for her newest drink.

Beau watched as she folded herself into her seat, tucking one foot under her and swinging the seat from side to side. There was something so… free about her. Loose.

Beautiful.

He couldn't tear his eyes away.

When she abruptly turned to the window and their eyes met, Beau stilled. Caught off guard, he offered a small wave. He had to bite back a laugh when she first looked behind her, confused, before returning the greeting.

With one small gesture, she'd reignited a hope he'd long lost.

Beau hadn't dated in over a year. Women wanted his status more than they wanted him. It walked into every room before he did, poisoned every relationship. Why date the man when you could court his money, power, and opportunity?

He was Beau Aaron Forrester, COO and heir.

Never *Beau*.

Maybe it was impossible. Most of his dreams had been.

But in an empty office on the twenty-fourth floor, sharing a smile with a beautiful stranger…

He'd trade every dollar he had for a chance to find out.

———

April stretched her arms behind her back, grimacing when her spine cracked in three places. *Oops.* Three was a bad sign. Maybe she should actually book an appointment with the chiropractor her mom was telling her about.

Back in January, when her promotion had come through, she'd had her boss sign off on an ergonomic chair and a sit/stand desk. It was all part of April's "work balance." New job; new healthy work habits.

Of course, the chair could only do so much when April spent eleven hours a day hunched over, glued to her dual monitors for the length of time it took to pass over an ocean.

The less said about the desk, the better.

"Confident people don't slouch" was her mom's favorite saying. Followed by "you shouldn't work so much." As though April's singledom was a result of her choosing her job over love.

Which she absolutely was.

But who needed proper posture — or a man — when on the verge of a breakthrough?

Now, if the data could just *get with the program,* that'd be perfect.

A pop-up on her screen flashed the bad news — the app had crashed again.

She combed her fingers through her hair, shaking off the loose strands that came after every wash.

She should call it a night. Even their international

office wouldn't be online for another six hours, and by that time, she'd be fast asleep.

What her mom failed to see was that April loved her job. She'd spent four years studying data science, then eight years working her way up into the digital advisor role. She wasn't going to give it all up to become someone's plus-one.

It wasn't that April didn't like men. She was simply... avoiding them.

Yes, she wanted love, but a result that certain required a lot of trial and error — bad date after bad date after bad date — April was happy to put it off a little longer.

So getting a crush on the gorgeous guy in the gray suit across the street was not ideal. Not that it was April's fault. It was completely unfair for *anyone* to be that attractive.

No. It was a terrible idea, and she would forget it.

She'd never see him again anyway. Chance City was full of guys in suits with a lot of ambition and no heart. If she ever found the time to date, she wanted more than that.

Finding a partner was the furthest thing from her mind right now. No matter how cute his wave was.

———

The Southbound Line was always quiet after nine p.m. Only a handful of people waited, all in various stages of exhaustion. As the train pulled in, April wrapped her scarf around her neck. It was only the first week of March, and the evening air still held a bit of bite.

These early days of spring held a promise of something special, like the cusp of a collective sigh. Looser smiles and lighter steps, the whole city ready and waiting for summer to arrive. Soon, sporadic rains would turn the air humid and sticky.

It was perfect.

The train car was empty as she took her seat, and when they pulled away from the station, only a single passenger sat across from her.

Shoulder length hair. Three-piece suit. Bone structure of a centerfold.

Oh.

From a distance, he'd been intriguing, but at close range… he packed a punch.

She'd seen the office across from her get cleared out, so she hadn't expected to see anyone there. And then, somewhere between escalating her fourth query error and making her fifth cup of coffee, there he was.

If the last guy had been a tornado of energy, he was a calm sea. Tousled brown waves down to strong shoulders and a trim waist — all of it wonderfully displayed in his tailored suit. Calling him fit felt like an understatement.

This man was scorching hot.

Molten lava in a three-piece.

He might as well have walked right out of April's dreams.

She hid her blush under her thick scarf.

When he'd given her that little wave earlier, he'd appeared sweet and, dare she say it, innocent.

Now he looked… well. Innocent was *not* how she'd describe him.

He was positively sinful.

Everything about him was perfectly in place, polished, down to the shine of his shoes. April surveyed her own tan boots with their scuffed heels and toes, the worn leather splattered with discoloration that she'd long since given up trying to clean off.

He really was something else.

Time passed while she admired him, searching for the cipher that would unravel his secrets.

The set of his mouth, tight and lopsided. His controlled posture. The unmistakable air of authority, as if he were a royal slumming it with his constituents.

But his eyes were what really captivated her.

Pale and overcast, the birth of storm clouds over the river.

Beautiful but lonely.

Who was he, with his expensive clothes and shrouded look? Where was he headed? Did he have someone at home to take the weight off his shoulders?

Did his carefully crafted exterior crack open when he laughed? Did those stormy blues ever brighten?

April's heart leaped into her throat when their eyes met. Without thinking, she wiggled her fingers, her mouth suddenly dry.

He smiled — just the slightest movement — an easy slide into dimple territory.

Whoa.

In a blink, she was racked with sensation, tingles spreading through her like wildfire. It reminded her of the starting climb of a rollercoaster, those first few seconds where her lungs filled with giddiness and anticipation.

Say something.

Overhead, the automated voice called out her stop. In seconds, she'd have to stand and leave. If she wanted to introduce herself, now was her last chance.

But she couldn't find her voice. She was rooted in place, mesmerized by the curl of his mouth, the kindness in his eyes.

Here was a man she could see herself with. She was overwhelmed with the need to know more about him.

If she could just open her mouth and *say something.*

"Doors closing."

She was out of time.

April tore out of her seat and darted out the doors.

Well, that was great. *Mom would be so pleased.*

His piercing gaze was still there when she turned back, but it was too late. The train was leaving and taking him with it.

Maybe the next time she saw someone cute, she could work up the courage to actually talk.

———

Beau's penthouse had always been too big for him. Vaulted ceilings, butler's pantry, a double-head shower he had no use for. Originally, the intention had been to fill the empty rooms, settle down, get three dogs.

It was a beautiful pipe dream.

Each breath came easier as he let the layers fall away, shrugging off his coat, jacket, and vest and throwing them onto an armchair as he crossed his living room. A sleek black turntable sat atop the sideboard, the largely bare shelving stocking his favorite albums and not much else.

Moving the needle into place, he set the record to play.

The bass rumbled deep under his feet, soaking into his bones, shaking out the frustration and loosening his spine. Beau turned it up, a smile easing onto his face, slow and steady as he returned to himself.

One advantage of living alone in a huge apartment was the fantastic acoustics.

Every day ended this way, with long, deep breaths and a groan. Shedding the hours of smug greetings, automated falsities, endless egotism. Every time he'd had to look someone in the eye and say, "I see your point," instead of "that's the dumbest fucking thing I've ever heard."

He undid the topmost buttons on his shirt while he reheated leftovers, stretching his neck as the noose slackened. Cooking was one of a long line of hobbies he never had time for anymore.

His whole life was a lot of *if only* suffocated under a metric ton of obligation.

JP's announcement loomed in his mind. Tomorrow, all eyes would be on him.

How many of them would be waiting for him to fail?

How many of them knew — as he did — that he wasn't cut out for it?

Distracted, he reached for his food but ripped his hand away when the plate burned his fingers. "Damn it."

"Hello? Is someone there?"

Beau spun, searching for whomever had spoken.

"I'm not sure how you got in —"

"Got in? This is my apartment; how did you get in? And where are you?"

Brow furrowed, he braced himself against the counter. What the hell was going on?

A quick pass through his apartment confirmed he was alone. Which meant the voice he was hearing... was inside his head.

With the heels of his hands, Beau rubbed at his eyes. It was completely impossible and yet, there she was, clear as day.

"Oh my god, you're in my head. The hell? I don't understand..."

Beau took a deep breath. "That makes two of us."

He really was hearing voices. Maybe he needed to restart his therapy sessions. It might be fun to talk about something other than JP for once.

"Are you still there?"

"Yes. I mean, I think so?"

He chuckled. "Okay, good."

"So… we can just … talk to each other? How is that possible?"

Beau blinked down at his dinner, his appetite gone. "I have no idea. This hasn't happened to me before."

"And here I was hoping you were the expert."

Huh. He hadn't expected her to be funny. He hadn't expected anything at all. Was he really about to accept a disembodied voice on top of everything else? Without even calling a doctor?

He gripped the bench, knuckles white. Why the hell not?

"Can you hear my thoughts? What number am I thinking?"

"Twelve?"

"Twelve? Your guess is twelve?"

"It's not twelve?"

Beau moved back to the living room. He needed to sit for this. "No, it was sixty-one. The year my dad was born."

"Hey, my dad was born in sixty-two. So I guess that's a no on the mind-reading question."

"I guess so," he said. Meaning they could only hear what was said aloud… Good to know.

"Maybe you're just my imagination. Tell me something I don't know."

Oh good, something easy… "Did you know that a quarter of all male black swans have same-sex relationships?"

"How do you even know that?"

"I wanted to be a vet when I was a kid."

"Vets need to know the sexual preference of swans?"

She was smiling, he was sure of it. He almost expected her voice to echo. Instead, it was steady and clear, like a lover speaking gently beside him, intimate and unguarded. It slipped easily under his clothes, between his ribs, loosening the last of the tension within him.

He took in the empty room around him, tried to imagine her sitting with him. "I wanted to work in a zoo. I was obsessed. As a kid, I spent all my time reading up on animal facts."

"You are something else." She laughed.

It was the oddest sensation, hearing her laugh like an echo in his own mind. Especially one so unfamiliar. The bright, lyrical sound trickled down his spine like a caress. He had to steady himself.

"I'm not even sure I could have made that up."

The smile he'd been fighting spread quickly then, muscles shifting like tectonic plates under his skin, lifting his cheeks, creasing the corners of his eyes.

He was hooked.

———

It took eight paces to get from one end of April's studio to the other.

What it lacked in space, it made up for by being affordable and close to her parents. But right now, it was downright claustrophobic.

"So what should I call you?"

"Oh! Right, I'm April." She twisted the rings on her right hand, thumbing over them in order. Index, middle, ring, pinkie. Then back again.

"Nice to meet you, April. I'm Beau."

Beau. She liked it. "Nice name. Kind of reminds me of old detective novels. There was always a rich, handsome guy called Whit or Kent whose fiancée was in trouble." Someone dapper. Broody. "Are you anything like that?"

His deep sigh rumbled like thunder, so different from her own voice it startled her.

"Can I be honest about something?"

"Please."

The silence that followed lasted for so long, April wondered if their connection had died. Without him standing in front of her, it was hard to tell.

Then his whiskey-rich voice returned. *"I'm going to sound like an asshole, and I really don't want you to think that, but my last name is pretty recognizable where I live, and I don't often get the opportunity to meet someone who doesn't know who I am before they get to know me, so if you don't mind, I'd like to get to know you without all of that. So maybe no last names or identifying details."*

Curiosity lit up the corners of her mind, the lure of a mystery beckoning, but April shut it down.

She knew all about living up to expectations. Or *not* living up to them, in her case. If Beau wanted a bit of anonymity, she could do that for him.

It wasn't as if they'd ever meet.

"Of course. Everything else is on the table?"

"*As much as you can handle,*" he said.

"Color me intrigued," she responded, delighting in the laugh that returned.

Oh, this would be fun.

Chapter Two

Beau had woken with the remnants of his dreams falling away like droplets of water on glass. Her voice echoed in all of them.

In all likelihood, she was a figment of his imagination, induced by the increased stress he was under, but he was drawn to her anyway.

People were rarely comfortable around him, too concerned with getting on his good side and never assured enough to be themselves or take the time to get to know who he really was.

Even though he hated it, wearing the persona had become habit.

But to April, he could be himself.

He caught his reflection in the elevator, a grin clinging to the corner of his lips.

Every morning, he woke, dressed in what he'd set out the night before, checked the news over a coffee, and started on his emails during the commute. Every step reconstructed the armor he'd removed the night before. It straightened his shoulders, blanked his gaze, and got him battle ready.

His smile was carefully hidden by the time he'd walked into his father's office.

"You're late," JP barked without looking up.

The man had two offices — one public, one private. The public one operated as a sitting room and meeting space. Comfortable furnishings softened sharp words, like a wolf in a wool coat.

Every morning, without fail, they'd have coffee and check in. Beau would love to *check out*.

"Sorry, I was polishing my son of the year award."

With a blink, JP set his sights on Beau, a signature movement full of disappointment.

He slipped into the leather armchair across from his father, accepting the black coffee that had been prepared for him by JP's assistant, Jeanine, before she slipped silently out of the room.

What was there to say about Jonathon Patrick Louis Forrester that hadn't already been covered by thirty or so news outlets and at least three biographies?

A tall, thin man, his father had always maintained a commanding presence. Even now, six months after his diagnosis, as his cheeks sank further and his hands began to twitch, his steely gaze and unwavering expectations hadn't lost their potency.

"You've seen the announcement, I hope." JP adjusted his glasses. Thin, wire rims that amplified his glare.

"I did."

"Good. I expect you to run the executive summary meeting on Friday."

Good morning, son. How are you?

Wonderful, actually. I met someone interesting last night…

Beau eased out a sigh. JP would never change.

"I'll have Rebecca update my calendar."

There was no indication his father heard him.

"Here." He set a record — one so fresh the plastic was still wrapped — on the desk between them.

Here was the thing about JP. The Company — capitals required — was his only love. He knew every intimate detail about their share price but had never once remembered Beau's birthday.

And yet. Ever since he'd discovered Beau listening to Miles Davis, he'd begun this odd ritual of randomly gifting LPs of artists Beau had never heard of.

He assumed each was a recommendation from whichever music store JP frequented. There was no chance Beau's seventy-year-old father knew who Christone "Kingfish" Ingram was.

By some miracle, most of his gifts were surprisingly good, so Beau's "thank you" was genuine.

It was an attempt, at least.

JP straightened, all business once again. "It's important that you manage this transition carefully. I'm not convinced you're prepared."

Well, that father-son moment was short-lived.

Beau sipped his coffee, letting the bitter sting satisfy his urge to snap back before swallowing it all down.

It didn't dissuade his father from continuing. Nothing ever discouraged JP. "There will be some who strive to undermine you. You can't let them."

"I'm aware of that."

"Then start doing something about it."

Beau released a hot breath through his nose, keeping his expression clear. Goading was JP's go-to strategy, whether it was business or parenting.

His father likely didn't know there was a difference.

He'd certainly never treated Beau differently from his other employees. Unless holding him to a higher standard counted. The organization was treated more lovingly than Beau ever had been, and the hierarchy hadn't escaped him. Beau would be lucky to make the top five of his father's priorities on any given day.

Beau doubted taking over the company would be enough to satisfy him. Hell, JP was a stubborn mother-fucker who'd probably haunt the building, like a modern-day, mean Jacob Marley.

Discarding his paper, JP stood, buttoned his suit coat, and left without a word.

Apparently, the conversation was over. Beau would really miss these heart-to-hearts.

Beau eyed the half-empty cup his father had left behind. "Good talk," he mumbled to the empty room.

"Someone isn't a morning person."

Suddenly, the day looked brighter. "I've been known to be a morning person when properly motivated."

"Kinky."

Damn, he could really like her if she kept this up. "Don't start anything you can't finish."

"What was that?"

Beau faltered at the sound of his father's voice from the doorway. "Nothing."

JP nodded and disappeared again. Beau quickly crossed to the other side of the eighty-fifth floor to his own office and closed the door behind him.

"Am I interrupting? I'm not sure how to shut this off, but I can be very, very quiet."

A smile spread before he could stop it. *Jesus,* barely five minutes with her, and he was eight again, talking to his first crush.

The soft, morning-warm tone of her voice coated her words and sent desire coursing straight to his cock. He was already sure he never wanted her to be quiet.

He'd need to pull himself together before the financial report this morning, or Bonnie would rake him over the coals.

"You're welcome to interrupt me anytime. You saved me from my father's morning roundup of disappointments."

"I'm sorry."

"I'm used to it. How can I take over the family business if he doesn't point out every way I'm failing?"

"There's a lot of anger there."

He let the silence linger, three decades of emotion pressing on his tongue, too large to swallow back. It wasn't something he liked talking about. Hell, most of his friends had no idea besides one, and Keaton wasn't here.

The number of people Beau could open up to was too small to count.

"I don't hate my father. I don't always like him, but it's been a long time since I wanted to outright hate him either. The year after I graduated was the worst — I screamed at him, he called me a disappointment, I said he could go fuck himself, and we didn't talk for two years."

"But you work together now…"

"Hmm."

"If you didn't make up with him, why did you decide to take over?"

And… *oh.*

Not a lot of people would have picked up on that.

Beau closed his eyes. Good business practice involved taking calculated risks. Over the years, he'd honed his instincts, learning to rely on his gut. And right now, it was telling him to trust her.

He wanted April to be real.

He wanted a lot of things.

"My father… He's dying, and I'm it." The responsibility of thousands of workers and billions of dollars would rest on Beau's shoulders soon. No matter how he felt about JP, he didn't take that lightly. "I always knew I would take over. It's simply happening sooner than I expected."

"I'm sorry."

So was he.

"You don't have to tell me about it if you don't want to. It's too early for me to be prying anyway. I've got twenty minutes to catch the train, and I'm still trying to motivate myself to get up."

Beau perked up. That meant they were in the same time zone, right? Dare he hope they could even be in the same city?

He checked the time. "It's almost seven, and you aren't up yet?"

"Excuse you. Some of us don't have to take tea with dear old Dad before the sun rises."

He chuckled.

"Wait. It's seven where you are too?"

Beau's heart beat a little faster. "Guess we're closer than we thought."

It sat on the tip of his tongue to ask her where she was. Which was reckless. As intriguing as she was, they barely knew each other. Actually, they *didn't* know each other.

But for the first time in years, he had something, someone, in his life that wasn't about influence and had nothing to do with his last name.

Of course he wanted more.

"Good morning, boss."

Beau looked up as his assistant, Rebecca, walked in. She wore a fitted black turtleneck over flared green trousers and stilettos. In one hand, she held a coffee. Her tablet in the other. She didn't wait for his reply before starting on his meeting schedule.

"— then you have the People and Capabilities follow-up at ten thirty. I rescheduled your meeting with

Bonnie for this afternoon because JP requested you attend the joint venture update instead."

Rebecca raised a shrewd brow over her coffee cup. "Unless you're otherwise indisposed at that time?"

It went without saying that Rebecca was one of Beau's favorite people. And one hell of an assistant.

"Please tell my father that unfortunately there is insufficient time to reschedule my obligations, but I'll ensure that I'm available at that time in the future."

"*Most of that was bullshit, wasn't it?*"

He coughed into his hand to hide the laugh. "Mm-hmm."

It was impossible to keep a straight face while April laughed freely, and when Rebecca caught his expression, she paused and studied him for a moment, then continued as if nothing had happened. But the glint in her eye said she'd noticed.

———

April could already smell the passata, the sweet earthiness of nutmeg wafting up the stairway. As much as she loved her parents, she was glad she didn't live with them anymore — her mom's cooking was amazing, but the meals were always paired with a deep dive into her love life.

When she reached the third-floor landing, she paused and sent off a quick reply to Henri. After the success of last week's pilot, she was eager to scale her analytics model. Eventually, it would need to handle six million lines of data code, but the project was in the early stages.

An idea had hit her on the walk here, but if her mom caught her sending a work email after five, she could kiss her dinner goodbye.

When she finally walked in, Helena was bent over a large pot.

"Hey, Mom."

April had gotten a lot from her dad — his pointed nose, thin hair, and sense of humor — but her intense focus came directly from her mom.

Helena whipped around, her pixie white hair bouncing with the movement. "Oh good. You're here! My phone isn't working."

April ditched her bag and jacket as the device was shoved into her face. No amount of explaining the difference between data science and IT could convince her mom that she wasn't a tech genius.

"I spent two hours on the phone with support earlier, and they knew nothing."

With a deep inhale, April unlocked the phone. Her mom should really stop using her birthday as a lock code.

"Why do you have three calendar apps?"

"One is for you kids, the other is for holidays and such, and the last one is for my workouts."

Oh, well, *that* made complete sense.

"Look at you. You're as bad as Felix," Helena said, brushing hair off April's shoulders with pursed lips.

Felix, having heard his name, scampered in, his little

legs motoring to get his fluffy body across the room in record speed.

"Let's hope your future husband likes dogs."

April's cheeks ran hot, and she focused very hard on the kitchen backsplash when her mom's gaze zeroed in on them.

"You don't need different apps for that. You could just make separate categories."

Helena clapped. "Fantastic. You can show me once you've fixed the SOS thing."

Great. There went April's evening. "What SOS thing?"

Forty excruciating minutes later, April excused herself from the kitchen. Fixing the problem had taken all of sixty seconds — simply popping the SIM card out and turning it the right way up — but explaining the issue had been an event. One would think April had invented cell phones by the way her mom volleyed questions at her.

Her dad, Scott, was already settled in his favorite armchair, television remote resting in his hand to mute ads before they had a chance to play.

His face was a time capsule of laughter. Deep lines bracketed his eyes and mouth, evidence of his good humor. Since his hip replacement a year ago, he didn't get around as much as he liked, but his mind was as sharp as ever.

"No, no. Don't get up," April joked, bending down to kiss her father on the cheek.

"Who am I getting up for? Is someone important

here?"

April dropped into the chair beside him, trying not to notice how labored his breathing had become.

Her heart clenched as he reached over and patted her hand. "What do you know?"

"We just finished the pilot this week. I still need to go through the results, but I have enough data to fine-tune the model now."

He smiled, his features soft with age, cheeks rosy from warmth in the room and the spitting image of Santa (minus the beard).

"I never doubted it. You always were the smart kid."

"Must have gotten that from Mom," April teased, laughing when her dad tsked.

"Be nice to your mother. She's having a rough time."

"What was it this week?" she asked. Helena loved a crusade almost as much as she loved nagging April. "An egg shortage? Did Isla petition for her stall again?"

Her dad frowned. "The fundraiser didn't reach their goal. The markets will have to close."

Shit. "How short are they?"

Scott ducked his head, confirming they were still alone. "They've got enough to keep going until May, but no longer than that."

Two months. No wonder her mom was upset.

April stole a look into the kitchen, where her mom was singing to herself, but the sag of her shoulders gave away her hurt.

Helena had been manning a stall at their local markets since before she'd met Scott. And they'd been an important part of the community for even longer. Without them… well, April knew what it was like to put your heart and soul into something. To see that end?

It would be heartbreaking.

———

April spent most of dinner ignoring her mom's loving jabs at her job. It wouldn't be nice to ruin a good meal by arguing.

But it was a close thing.

April got it, she *did*. Family was everything to her too, but surely Helena, who had turned their spare room into her pottery studio, could understand what April would be missing if she set aside her career.

She'd worked so hard, and she was only twenty-seven. She still had time.

"Honey, you should be out meeting people. Ever since you took that promotion, all you do is work."

"It's a chance of a lifetime. Do you know how few companies ROBA collaborates with on automation? How rare it is for a non-engineer to even get a look in? I couldn't pass this up. And it's not forever. The project wraps up in six months."

Of course, then April would have the opportunity to apply directly for work with them, but her mom didn't need to know that.

"You can do that later. You only have so long to have children." Her mom pulled another hair off April's sweater.

April said nothing.

"Oh, your sister called. She needs someone to babysit tomorrow night."

Subtle.

"Did Ruby say what time I should be there?"

Of course she would do it. She always did.

"Oh, thank you, honey. The boys will love that."

It was harder not to keep her mouth shut when her mom looked at her pointedly and said, "You'll have your own soon."

———

April loved having her own space most of the time.

Growing up, she'd wondered what it would be like to live in an actual house. Kids on TV had their own rooms, whereas April had shared everything. Squeezing four kids and two adults into an apartment had meant things like privacy were nonexistent until she'd left for college.

Not having to share a bathroom was the height of luxury.

But that didn't stop her from being lonely.

Waking at the same hour, night after night, there was nothing to do except think. No chores she could convince herself were worth getting out of bed for, no mindless entertainment she wanted to distract herself with.

Not that she ever had time for it — the only shows she watched were her dad's favorite mysteries on Friday nights and the cartoons her nephews loved. Right now, they were obsessed with some old show about gargoyles. It was actually pretty entertaining.

April rolled over, pulling the duvet up to her chin.

If she went to sleep now, she'd still manage five hours before her alarm went off. Five hours was okay.

Too bad her mind was wide awake.

"Go to sleep," she whined.

But it turned out she wasn't the only one awake at two a.m.

"I was wondering when I'd hear from you again."

Her whole body was awake now, her heart jumping into her throat and a buzzing kicking off just beneath her skin.

April smiled into her pillow. "Wondering or hoping?"

"Absolutely hoping," Beau said.

April blushed. So had she.

As her eyes adjusted to the dim light of the room, blacks faded into grays. She slid a hand across her mattress, feeling the indents below the sheet, tracing their lines and remembering how it had felt to have the heat of someone beside her.

It had been a long time since she'd wanted to fill that space.

"What do you look like?"

"Is this your way of asking me what I'm wearing?"

Oh god, was she? April's body flushed hot beneath her covers, and she wrapped them tighter around herself. Desire pulsed between her thighs, making her wet.

If he asked, would she admit that she slept naked?

"Maybe," she whispered, then thought better of it. "I want to picture your face."

"Blue eyes, kind of beady. Big forehead, long hair."

She laughed. "This is you trying to impress me?"

His voice was low. *"It's not working?"*

How could he, with so few words, get to her like this? Casually coax a blush with only his voice?

She gripped the duvet, resisting the urge to cover her cheeks.

"Now you."

"Um," she wrestled to get a hold of herself. "Brown hair, brown eyes. I think my nose is a little small for my face, and I have a dimple in my chin."

She turned onto her back, hand on her chest. She'd never had to describe herself before. What would he think?

In the nicest way possible, her body was an arithmetic mean — average in every way.

"My mom calls me short, but that's only because my brothers and sister got her height. I don't know what else to say… I like my smile," she admitted.

"You sound beautiful."

Her eyes closed, and she held on to his voice, safely storing it away in her rainy-day fund.

"Then you're picturing the wrong thing," she teased.

"No, I'm picturing you. And I'm not talking about your looks,

even though that doesn't change my answer. I'm talking about your voice."

Her breath caught. Under her fingers, her heart jumped around like an excited puppy.

How was Beau even *real?*

His voice was rough and smooth all at once, like crunchy peanut butter sticking to the inside of her mind, coating every inch of her body with warmth. Desire.

"I…" She paused, breathless. What could she even say to that?

"People tend to only see the outside. I like getting to know what's underneath."

Her gut twisted at his casual acceptance of being treated as a pretty thing that people objectified. What kind of life was that?

"Is this your way of asking me what *I'm* wearing?" she asked, mirroring his teasing from earlier.

"Only if you want to tell me." The interest in his voice was unmistakable.

"Maybe next time," she said. Heat sizzled in her veins, and she whipped the sheet off, needing a second to cool down. "It's been a while since anyone has wanted to see underneath." *Geez.* Why did everything sound so suggestive? "Do you know what I miss about dating?"

"What's that?"

So many little things. A kiss. Having someone to split dessert with. Rolling over to share someone's warmth, tangling her limbs with theirs, knowing they'd be there when she woke up. When she got home.

When she needed them most.

"I miss cuddling. Getting really close, breathing someone in. I could spend hours just lying around, existing together."

These were things she usually didn't say. It was too honest, too transparent, and she was terrified it would turn a guy off. But it was easier from a distance. Or maybe it was because it was *Beau*.

"Christ, I know what you mean. You know what I miss? When you're not necessarily doing anything special, but you look up or look over, and they're there, and it's almost painful how much you want them because it barely fits inside you. Words don't seem like enough to even express it, so you keep looking, hoping you can find some way of showing them. Is it possible to miss a feeling you've never had?"

The world had stopped, her whole body becoming a reverberating drum. She could feel her heartbeat in her *lips*.

Only after a few steadying breaths did she trust herself to speak.

"I think so." Of that she was certain.

The question burst forth before she could stop it. "Where are you right now?"

"Are you sure this isn't a booty call?"

She had never been more thankful that he couldn't see her. Her face was on fire.

"I couldn't help myself. Actually, I'm glad you asked. I know I said no details, but I'm really hoping you live in Chance because I like knowing you're close by."

"I do."

He was here. In her city. He was out there right now, under the same stars, thinking of her. She could have passed him on the street, brushed by him on the train or at work. "So…"

"Yes?"

"What *are* you wearing?"

Two a.m. didn't seem so bad anymore.

Chapter Three

"This is the data from this week."

Another slide.

"The green bar represents…"

Unbelievable. Forty minutes into this meeting and only now were they getting to the point. Beau took a deep breath while Doug droned on.

What was April doing right now?

"What drives the use of the calendar days?" Bonnie asked. "It's unfair to metricize a five-day-a-week business around a seven-day calendar."

It had only been a week since they'd met, and Beau couldn't stop thinking about her.

He blinked, his eyes tired and dry after a night of little sleep. They'd talked for hours. It had been worth it, even if he felt like reheated leftovers.

What part of the city was April looking at right now?

Beau's office had one of the best views in the city,

and yet he never had the opportunity to enjoy it. What was the point of having a desk at the top of the mountain if he spent all his time locked away in the caves?

"Our process has already been tested, and now we're expanding that knowledge —"

Bonnie cut in, leaning across the table. "I'm not arguing the approach, what I'm trying to highlight…"

The sun was out for the first time in weeks, teasing Beau as it glinted off the neighboring buildings. He'd love to be out there, breathing in the fresh ocean air that blew in across the harbor.

The presentation was stuffed full of graphs and predictions but had nothing real to say. Doug was explaining how combining branding campaigns across previously unlinked industries *blah, blah, blah*.

He used to pay more attention. Back straight, ears open. Taking notes on everything from the engagement level in the room to the number of slides and the presentation style of each speaker, hoping it would make him a better leader.

It had. Beau might not have chosen any of this for himself, but he gave a damn, and Forresters were nothing if not stubborn creatures.

But none of that mattered. Because no one cared whether he was a good leader. They only needed an audience to perform for.

That's all it ever was. A performance.

Only the hardest working people in the room — limited to their CFO, Bonnie, and Beau — didn't treat their careers like a corporate pageant.

"Would you just work? If you make me go to the tech café one more time, I swear I will rip out every single one of your keys."

The obvious exacerbation in April's voice brought a smile to Beau's face. "Problem?"

"Beau! Oh, the usual. I'm going to murder my laptop."

The sound of a throat clearing grabbed his attention, and every eye in the room was on him. Right. The meeting. "Sorry, I was thinking out loud. Keep going."

After a confused pause, Doug continued.

"Where are you? A meeting?"

"Yes," he said, avoiding Bonnie's gaze. Whatever he'd agreed to with that response better not bite him in the ass later.

"Interesting… so I can say anything I want, and you can't reply?"

"Mm-hmm."

Bonnie narrowed her eyes. "Beau? Something to add?"

He searched the graphs displayed behind Doug, desperate for something to help him recover. "Actually, I was curious about the, uh…"

Bonnie frowned.

Shit. Beau wasn't an "uh" person. Too much good breeding.

None of that stopped the suggestive little voice in his ear.

"Intimate synergies? If the current approach is too hard, maybe you need to bang out the details. Give the bottom line a good tongue lashing."

A cough was startled out of him. Jesus *Christ.* Thank

fuck for the table, because his body hadn't gotten the memo that now was not the time. His cock was far too interested in April's little spiel.

He'd have time to be embarrassed later. For now, he needed to stop imagining April and his tongue in the same room and start climbing out of this hole.

"Beau?"

"The hard line," he choked out, a flush creeping up his neck. Even his ears felt warm.

"Excuse me?"

He was going to lose this job before he even had it.

After a deep breath, Beau straightened. "You mentioned exploring value creation to offset the bottom line. Could you expand on that point?"

More than one person was still eyeing him oddly. He adjusted, resting his chin on his hand so he could cover his mouth.

Doug nodded. "Of course. If we go to the next slide —"

"You sound good when you're giving orders. Very sexy. I bet you look the part too. Have I told you how much I like a man in a suit?"

"Interesting…" he said, his voice low. He hoped it made sense against whatever Doug was waffling on about, but honestly, he didn't have a clue, and he absolutely didn't care.

April chuckled. God, her voice…

"I should go… let you get back to your hard line."

It still didn't make sense, how this had all come about, but Beau wouldn't look a gift horse in its telepathic mouth. Whatever this was, April was angel and devil both, tempting him in all the right ways.

"Beau, anything to add?"

His head shot up. Bonnie — and the rest of the room — waited, all eyes on him once again.

Where should he start?

The last strategy and planning meeting where he'd been outvoted from increasing benefits for their staff because executive bonuses would have been affected? Or he could mention how delays in this very development had already cost them millions — the same millions he'd been denied investing in public school programs. Maybe he should bring up his favorite topic — sustainability — and they could explain why they still weren't meeting their CO_2 goals.

But what was the point? He wasn't here to shake things up. He was here to be JP junior. Simply nod and sign.

Bonnie waited, her polite smile a patented trick he'd seen employed with ruthless precision. It was incredibly effective and a little scary, much like her.

He sighed. "How do you plan on offsetting the recent increase in steel price?"

As Doug geared up to answer, Beau knew he wouldn't be leaving any time soon.

———

If you'd asked April what she wanted to be as a kid, she'd probably have said something like a detective or a royal advisor, because they were very serious and important jobs that involved solving problems and striding confidently into rooms.

She would not have said data analyst.

April had been hoping to transition out for a few years, once her graduate program had ended, perhaps taking what she'd learned and going into renewable energy like some of her colleagues. But without an engineering background, the choices were slim.

That was why this robotics collaboration meant so much to her.

Henri MacLeod's automation project was basically her pot of gold.

"The initial data is looking good," Henri said.

He stood at ease in front of the mounted whiteboard, his complicated scribbles — the only handwriting April had seen that was worse than hers — making sense only to the two of them. His posture was intimidating, as was his reputation, but the silvering at his temples and his obsession with licorice and blue jeans had been paramount in stopping April from hyperventilating every time she remembered who she was working with.

"I'll recommend that we start phase three when I meet with the VP on Friday."

"But we haven't finished our current sprint." Sure, the data supported her theory, but wasn't more evidence better than less?

"We can run them concurrently. After I pass on this morning's results, I'm confident we'll get the budget we need to stand up a small team to prototype."

Holy shit. That was big.

He popped the whiteboard marker back in its spot with a flick of his wrist, nodding into the middle distance the way her father did sometimes when he was concentrating.

"Don't get your hopes up just yet. It can be tempting to think a few good results are the sign of a stable solution, but the one thing I've learned in my career is to pay as much attention to your failures as your successes. That's growth right there." He snagged one last licorice bite and moved to the doorway. "You have a lot of potential, and you're smart. Let's just take it one day at a time."

Excitement fizzed under her skin. As soon as he'd passed through the doorway, she spun in her chair and allowed herself one small squeal.

Suddenly, the future opened up, plans colliding in her thoughts, jumping over themselves for space. If this went well, then in six months to a year, she could look at moving to a better place. Maybe she could start saving and take that trip to the coast she'd always wanted.

She wondered if Beau liked big boats and portside cocktails.

———

April cradled the phone on her shoulder as she typed. She would not whine. "But why?"

41

"Because I'm your mother, that's why, and you aren't doing anything about it yourself."

"That's because I'm too busy. Where did you find him anyway?"

"Don't say it like that. Dylan is Priscilla's nephew, and he's perfectly nice. Which you'll find out when you meet him for dinner tonight."

"I can't believe you set me up on a date without telling me. What if I'd had a work meeting?"

"Do you?"

April twisted her mouth. The urge to lie was strong. But she couldn't. "No."

"Wonderful. He'll meet you at La Delizia at eight."

She'd say yes, of course. It would be rude not to. But she didn't have to be happy about it.

"He offered to pick you up from your apartment, but I know how you get with those old-fashioned gestures."

"Mom, I'm being safe. Or would you rather I give every man in the city a key to my apartment?"

"Of course not. Look at what happened the last time you tried to live with someone."

Of course she would bring up Preston. April waited until she'd hung up to groan loudly.

What her mom didn't understand was that the gesture wasn't the problem. Chivalry, when it was genuine, was welcome. But inviting a man to her apartment — showing him where she lived — meant letting him into her life. And history had proven that to be disastrous.

So it was safest to keep a distance until she knew if he could be trusted.

April stared longingly at her laptop.

There were twenty unread emails in her inbox and an ROT analysis she'd planned to run tonight. Instead, she would have to leave before five, remember how to do her date makeup, hope her unwashed bun wasn't too casual, and then spend a few hours making awkward small talk with a stranger her mother picked out.

She pushed away from her desk and searched for her favorite suit model across the street. But the neighboring office was empty.

"Where are you?"

"Looking for me?"

Her heart skipped. It had a habit of doing that whenever Beau appeared. "What if I was?"

"You found me. You have interesting timing. Caught me in the locker room with no pants on."

"Are you… I mean, um." Her neck was burning with embarrassment. The only comfort was knowing Beau couldn't see it.

She could, however, hear the satisfaction in his voice.

"What are you thinking about, April?"

"Nothing."

"I don't believe you."

"That's too bad."

"It really, really is."

April grabbed the first piece of paper she could and fanned herself with it. She had never — never — done anything like this at work. She didn't even know what they were doing. Only what she wanted.

"What's happening right now?"

"April? Are you talking to me?" Henri's head popped through the frame of April's *open* office door. It was official: her face would be stuck in a permanent blush.

"Oh, uh, no. Sorry. I'm, uh, the phone."

"Oh my gosh, of course! Didn't mean to interrupt."

"Everything okay over there?"

April cringed behind her hands. "My coworker slash boss just caught me talking to myself."

"I should go. Maybe we can finish this later."

"Um, I'm actually going on a date tonight. Something my mom set up."

He went quiet.

April whacked herself with the paper. Rule number one of dating — don't tell the guy you really like that you have a date with someone else. No wonder she was single.

"Well. Good luck with your date."

Chapter Four

April tapped a finger on the wooden table, then adjusted the tea light for the fifth time. She wouldn't check her emails.

It had been her mantra since she'd put her phone into her purse, but as the seconds ticked by, her nerves had only risen, and she needed a distraction before she talked herself into leaving.

"It's one date," she whispered. "You can do this."

"Nervous?"

April's heart skipped when Beau's rich voice sounded in her mind, and she scanned the room to be sure no one was looking in her direction before she responded. "First dates are awful. I got so jittery sitting at my apartment, but now I've been waiting here for twenty minutes. The staff keeps giving me pity looks."

Beau's rumble of laughter reverberated through her, and she covered her growing smile with her hand, tracing the grain of the wood with one finger.

"It's going to be fine. You're intelligent, charming, beautiful," he said.

April happily rolled her eyes. No matter how much she protested, Beau wasn't deterred. At least he hadn't suggested they meet. April couldn't stand to disappoint him.

"Just be yourself. If anyone should be nervous, it's him."

"April?"

April looked up to find her date's rounded face and kind eyes. He wore a gray business shirt and black pants, his hand outstretched.

"Hi, I'm Dylan."

Cute *and* polite. No wonder her mother had given her blessing. April bet he had a safe and appropriate job, too, like an accountant or a branch manager. Not that it would matter.

Preston had been a workforce coordinator — a fancy term for HR rep. He'd had career progression ahead of him, savings in the bank, and a short list of kids' names.

In the end, it was April who hadn't measured up.

In a perfect equation, she was an anomaly.

He pulled his hand back and slid into the seat across from her before April could respond. "Wow, your mother said you were beautiful, but I didn't really believe her. It's what everyone says, you know? But she was right."

"Um." April hesitated. Had she been out of the game for too long? What should have been a compliment sounded more like an insult, but she should probably give him the benefit of the doubt. Especially if she wanted to still be on good terms with her mom next week. "Thanks?"

"I'm usually the early one, but you managed to beat me. When I heard you were a workaholic, I thought maybe you might. I don't know about you, but late people really piss me off. So it's good you weren't."

Maybe she'd only order an appetizer. She wasn't that hungry, anyway.

"He's there, isn't he?"

Oh, no.

"Mm-hmm," April quietly replied, then cleared her throat. Now she had to date with an audience? She was totally about to embarrass herself.

Dylan's head hadn't stopped nodding since he'd arrived. He could probably be on this date by himself.

Keeping her hands busy, April took a sip of water. "So, um, you're a dentist? What's that like?"

"He's a dentist? April, April, April. If he makes a tooth pun, promise me you'll never see him again."

She bit back a smile.

Dylan picked up the menu, still nodding. "It's good. You could almost say it's tooth-riffic."

Water rushed into her airway as she choked on a laugh, coughing and spluttering.

Dylan reared back, his eyes wide, fixing his frown on the spilled water and then on her. "Are you okay?"

She nodded, blinking back tears. Beau was going to pay for that.

"Maybe you should clean up in the bathroom. It's just, people are staring."

If April hadn't been busy trying to breathe, she would have told him where to put his concerns for *other people*. To think she could have been running queries tonight, but *no*, she was on the world's most awkward three-way date.

With a forced smile, she pushed up from the table and made her way to the bathroom, catching a sympathetic smile from the waitress as she passed.

The food here better be terrible because April was never coming back.

She blanched at her reflection. Her cheeks were on fire, and dark smudges framed her eyes. At least no one else was around to witness as she buried her face in her hands.

"How's the date going?"

He should be glad she didn't know where to find him.

April whipped her head up. "Terrible, thanks to you. I just choked on my water."

"Which one did he use?"

"Tooth-rrific." April braced her hands on the sink, taking in her flustered expression. What was she doing? Even if Dylan did turn out to be nice, she didn't want to be there. "I don't know why I let my mom talk me into this. I have a presentation to read through, at least three formulas are broken, and I'm the only one who doesn't freak out over using V-Lookups with boolean expressions, and yet here I am, talking to myself in a public bathroom, hiding from my date."

"You're extremely sexy when you're in work mode. Did you know that?"

"Beau," April chided. Being turned on by someone who wasn't her date was bad form. *Bad, April.* "That's not helping."

"Good. I don't want to help. Maybe I want to sabotage your date with the dentist so I can keep you to myself."

Tingles spread from April's fingers, along her arms, and up her neck, leaving goose bumps in their wake. Of course she'd rather be on a date with him. He'd probably bring flowers to her door and kiss her cheek and then do something completely romantic like cook her dinner.

But it wasn't Beau sitting at that table, waiting for her to come back. It was Dylan. And it wasn't fair for her to wish he was someone else.

She straightened, dabbed cool water on her neck, and made her way back to the table. It was one date. How hard could it be?

"So, Dylan. Why dentistry?"

"I bet he can't even make you laugh. What does dentist of the year get? A little plaque."

April nodded while Dylan talked, hearing nothing. She tipped both corners of her mouth into a smile, praying he wasn't telling her a story about how his childhood pet had passed or the time he'd fallen down a well.

"What does a dentist do on a rollercoaster? He braces himself."

She tried her best to ignore Beau, her gut shaking with the force of holding back her reaction.

"You haven't said anything in a few minutes, so I can only assume that this guy is still *talking. Which, if you asked me, is a huge red flag."*

April bit on the inside of her cheek to stop herself from laughing.

"If I were him, I'd be too interested in you to talk about myself. I would want to know everything about you, and I'd hang on your every word. I'd ask myself, what did I do to deserve this incredible woman? I'd do whatever I could to make you laugh. To make you want me back. Enough to get a second date, and then a third, and on and on until you didn't want to see anyone else."

April's heart raced. She wanted that. More than anything.

She stood abruptly, her chair scraping along the ground. "I'm so sorry…"

Dylan stopped mid-sentence, frowning. "You need to leave, don't you? It's okay. You don't have to make up an emergency."

"I don't mean to brush you off, but —"

"Stop," she bit out, immediately regretting it when Dylan's expression fell further. This was awful. If there were awards for bad dates, tonight would win it. She'd be mortified for weeks, remembering the resigned crease in his brow.

"I'm so sorry, I didn't mean you…" She swallowed. This was why she didn't date. "I should go."

———

April took the long way home, letting the night air cool her heated skin. The sky was clear enough to walk home, and she breathed in the familiar smells of the city, brushing past people whose nights were just starting. Oddly, it wasn't lonely, knowing Beau was with her.

"I can't believe I just walked out." What was she going to tell her mom?

"I'm glad you did."

The rich, deep tone of his voice curled through her body, settling in her stomach, sliding lower.

"You don't have to sound so smug about it."

"He wasn't right for you. I am."

April cooled her heated cheeks with her icy fingers. "You can't be serious," she mumbled. He could have anyone he wanted. "Why would you want to date me? Clearly, I'm terrible at this."

"No one is terrible at dating."

"I am." She twisted her hands, rubbing them to ward off the night chill. The answer was obvious, even if Beau couldn't see it yet. "People rely on me to solve complex problems. I can take hundreds of thousands of rows of data and extrapolate a solution, but dating is a mystery to me."

When presented with a problem no one else could solve, the trick was to look for the key, the constant in a sea of chaos. What remained the same when the results varied?

The answer was *her*.

"It never works out," she admitted, bouncing on the balls of her feet as she waited for the light to change. "That's why I prefer my work. Something needs to be done? Work out the components and tick them off in order. Simple. But people? Relationships? They're messy, complicated. Emotional. I've never been good at being vulnerable."

It was easier to remove herself — simply delete the offending data, and hooray — an ideal outcome, for everyone except her.

"That's what makes us so good together. I have a long history of being too emotional."

She hid her laugh from the couple who passed by. It wasn't that she didn't want to date Beau. He was wonderful. Sweet, cocky, a little odd.

She liked him more than she had liked anyone in a long time, and more than she probably should, considering she didn't even know his last name or anything beyond how his voice settled something deep inside her.

It was clear he had a reputation — money too — but he never tooted his own horn. She'd dated more than one guy who'd worn his achievements as a chip on his shoulder. Whose compassion was a short string and who had never accepted April as she was.

Beau wasn't like that.

It was easier, somehow, to turn the deadbolt and invite him inside. He'd already gotten under her skin, in her lungs.

"Don't say that like it's a bad thing. It's why I like you."

What could it hurt, really? If it didn't work out, she could find some way of severing the tie that connected them, one that didn't corrupt the source.

"See? Perfect."

Chapter Five

Their long, late-night chats were becoming a regular occurrence, and after two weeks, Beau found himself coming home earlier, eager to get as much time with her as possible.

"How do you live without an oven?"

She laughed. *"Easy, I don't cook."*

"How do you eat?"

"I'm not sure if you've heard of them, but there are these newfangled contraptions called microwaves."

"That's a lot of sass from someone who doesn't know who Thom Pearson is."

"Because you made him up!"

"He's the biggest movie star on the planet. I can't believe you've never seen a single one of his films. *Another Sun? The Undeserving?*"

"Unless he's been on Detective Monroe, *you should give up now."*

Beau shook his head, setting the burger on a plate to

rest and charring a bun over the grill. His jaw ached from smiling. Behind him, Hank Mobley's version of "Deep in a Dream" played softly, the tenor floating in the air, sweeping and romantic.

It was difficult to remember another time he'd been so content.

"How about music?" he asked, plating the bun and stacking up his burger.

"I like music," she said, clearly determined to be as vague as possible. She did that a lot. *"You mentioned you like jazz. Who are your favorites?"*

He'd anticipated the question. April did that a lot too. Deflected attention.

"The classics, but they're a given. I've been listening to a lot of Stanley Jordan lately. He uses an interesting tapping technique that gives him a unique sound. It's pretty cool."

"Oh yeah? Is he a smooth cat?"

No one had ever teased him the way she did. He braced himself against the counter as he laughed, overcome with the need to hold her, to taste the smile he heard in her voice every night.

"There's a great bar on Prince Lane that features a jazz quintet on Sunday nights. I'll take you sometime."

"Oh yeah? What if I hate jazz? For all you know, my idea of a good night out is darts and terrible beer."

"As long as you're there, it'll be the best night of my life."

"I think you've been listening to too much Stanley Jordan."

Beau's laugh drowned out the music.

———

April rounded the other side of her bed and pulled the fitted sheet into place. Soft notes of lavender rose from the clean sheets. She couldn't wait to lie down.

"You made that up!"

He laughed again, smooth and silken. It was the best kind of remedy. Like slipping under thick blankets on a cold day.

"I swear it's true. You can look it up."

The last corner complete, she ran a hand over the material, the cotton soft under her palm. "I don't need to. I trust you."

"Do you?"

"Of course," she said. "Even if you are a figment of my imagination."

"Am I ever going to convince you this is real?"

April paused, a thrill zinging from her temple to her toes. She didn't need convincing. The last few weeks had been a dream, but it was more real than it had any right to be.

Certainly more real than what she'd had with Preston.

She stripped out of her clothes and slipped into bed. The sheets were cool and cozy and exactly as good as she knew they would be. She pressed her face against her pillow, whispering her secrets into the fibers. "Sometimes I think you're too good to be true."

When he spoke, his voice was softer than her sheets, making her shiver.

"If I could dream up the perfect person, it would be you."

The words kissed her skin. How could this *not* be a dream? No one had ever treated her the way Beau did, yet he'd never laid eyes on her.

The silence stretched out again.

"Beau?" She hugged her pillow tighter. Cocooned in the warmth of the blanket, her throat tight with feeling, she could almost convince herself she wasn't alone.

He hummed sleepily. His voice was fresh honeycomb and brandy, a deep rumble that swooped and swirled through her blood like mercury.

"Thank you."

"Sweet dreams, April."

―――――

March had disappeared in a blink. Beau's days had been filled with more meetings than he could stand, his nights made complete with April.

He'd never been happier or more miserable, his existence split between who he hoped to be and who he was, opposite in almost every way and unraveling his self-control.

The fresh air brought few answers, the sky murky enough that most people had chosen to stay inside.

In front of him, a couple walked their dog. Want wrapped itself around his lungs at the sight, squeezing.

When he thought about the future, he didn't see board meetings and press conferences. He wanted *that*. Two people, holding hands, in love.

Uncomplicated.

April deserved uncomplicated.

Without his money and his name, what did Beau have to offer? Was it a waste to hope that he'd be enough without it?

Out here, he was one of millions. A face in the crowd. Nobody special.

He could lose himself in the breadth of it.

It led him through the streets, wool coat turned up, his mind clear, the familiarity of the surrounding buildings a force field. His grandfather used to take him on long journeys through the town center, memories falling from his lips as they walked, almost all of them tied to his sweetheart, Maggie.

It had let Beau see Chance through his grandfather's eyes, and he'd fallen for the city just as George had — every cornice and alleyway a piece of the scrapbook showcasing who his grandfather had been and where Beau had come from.

One day he hoped to be that old man, sharing his heart with someone special. That dream had always seemed out of reach before.

Then April had appeared.

It was ridiculous to get attached; he knew that. They had just met. He shouldn't want to throw caution to the wind and tell her everything.

It was too soon, too needy. *Too emotional.*

Everything JP had been trying to train out of him.

———

"Stop it. I can't breathe," April wheezed out, the desk shaking under her as she braced against it. Beau's increasingly bizarre animal facts had sent her into a fit of giggles.

"Too much?" he asked, but the honey thickness of his smile was impossible to miss. She wanted to bathe in it.

Even though she knew the basics, she'd stopped trying to imagine the details of his face. Instead, she pictured his hands — undressing her, holding her — his breath on her neck, his lips on hers.

It didn't matter if he was a dream made real, as long as no one woke her up.

"My parents have a dog, Felix. He's a terror, but I love him."

"I've always wanted a German shepherd, but they shed a lot, so if you aren't careful, you'll be covered in it. My dad wasn't a fan."

"Why don't you get a pet? You clearly love animals enough, although I still don't think anyone needs to know the mating habits of hyenas in the detail you do…"

Beau chuckled.

"It wouldn't be right to put a pet through my life. Most days, I work twelve hours, and even when I'm not here, I can't avoid the constant emails. I skip lunches so I can work out and then live off what I can shove into my mouth between meetings. I don't have time for television, and I'm not on social media. My life is my job and any scant sliver of normalcy I can cobble together when I'm not in the office. I have enough money to set myself up for life, yet

I'll never enjoy it because I'll only ever see the inside of a boardroom."

"There's so much more to you than that, Beau." If only she had the right words, like Beau did. There was a deep sweetness about him, in the way that he listened and cared. "You don't equate what you have with your worth, and you don't judge others by that either. I can't imagine anything worse than seeing you lock that big heart of yours up simply to fulfill your father's expectations. You deserve to make your own dreams come true."

That night, April's dreams were filled with slow walks by the river, with Beau at her side and a puppy at their heels.

———

Beau stretched, tucking one arm under his pillow. Moonlight cast shadows across his ceiling above him, illuminating empty spaces and bare walls.

He let out a slow breath, rubbing at the persistent ache under his collarbone — the one that said *April is everything you've ever dreamed of* and *what are you waiting for?* "I wish I'd met you years ago. Where have you been my whole life?"

"I've been where I'll always be. Here for you."

His heart skipped a beat under his fingertips.

"Do you ever wish you'd had a brother or sister?"

He had once. But life was too short for the impossible. "Sometimes. JP is a lot to handle, and I haven't always had someone to talk to. I can't imagine having a big family."

"I love it, but being the baby isn't easy. Everyone else's mistakes become my blueprint. As though I'm going to repeat history, even though we're totally different people. There's a lot of pressure to do it right."

He knew that feeling. "Some nights I'd lie awake in bed dreaming of another life."

"If you really don't want to work there, why do you stay? Once your father's gone, can't you leave? You should be able to do anything you want."

It was a good question, and one he was having a hard time answering for himself. He used to tell himself it was familial pride, but the longer he watched JP slip away, the more Beau wondered who this was all for. Could he really stomach dedicating the rest of his life to his father's dream? How long would it take before he had given all of himself away?

The simple truth was that JP was the only family he had. Once he was gone, there wouldn't be anyone around who cared about Beau, even if his father had a shitty way of showing it. To wait until he had passed only to turn his back on it all felt callous, and not at all the kind of man Beau wanted to be.

"Like it or not, he is my family. I don't want to lie to him."

"But you already are."

He let out a harsh sigh, shifting on the bed. It was an awful truth. He'd been playing his role for so long that he'd stopped trying to justify it. Too many people expected things from him. At least with JP, he'd known how to pass the test.

But to give up on any other future... to be nothing more than a placeholder in the company's history, raising a son to fill his place someday...

"Does not having a relationship with your birth mom bother you?"

He shuffled on the bed, his heart heavy. "No. Renee is lovely, but we were never going to have that kind of relationship. She agreed to give JP a baby, and that's what she did."

Having a stranger for a mother had stung, but he never held it against her. His birth was an arrangement, a line item on the surrogacy contract. JP wanted a son, and he always got what he wanted.

"I really want to hug you right now. My mom drives me up the wall some days, but I can't imagine life without her. Maybe things would be different with her now?"

He took a deep breath. April meant well, but he didn't want to force a relationship with Renee where there wasn't one. They'd tried before, and it had only been awkward and uncomfortable. What he wanted — *needed* — was a family.

"The truth is, I didn't grow up with either of them. JP wasn't around at all, too busy running the company, but my grandfather made the effort when he could. He shared a lot of stories about the history of Chance, what parts of the city were from the original settlement, and how the Fo —" He cut himself off. *Shit.* He'd almost mentioned his family name. "How the first families built the city up."

He rubbed at his eyes, silently cursing.

"But if you'd had more of a connection to your mom, then you —"

"April. No." Beau's chest felt tight. "I know it might not make sense, but I don't need to change it."

Her voice was a whisper. *"Shit, I'm sorry."* Then louder, *"Beau, I didn't mean to imply... I guess I can't relate, and I was trying to, but that was out of line."*

He didn't want to fight, especially not about this. JP caused enough problems; he shouldn't be allowed to ruin this as well. And yet, when Beau played his own words back, all he heard was his father.

"I'm sorry too."

"It's exactly like what my mom does to me. Ugh. I promised myself that I would never do that."

Every day, Beau looked in the mirror and saw reminders of JP: the curve of a cheek, his brow.

"I'm terrified of becoming my father. He's not an emotional man, unless that emotion is disappointment. It's been a constant source of misery for him — how *much* I feel, how easily I let it lead me instead of being in control of it." JP had never minced words when it came to this particular flaw.

"You have nothing to worry about. I don't know him, but I know you, and you're incredible. You don't have to be what someone else wants. You only have to be you."

Would she say that if she knew who he *really* was?

"We don't always see eye to eye, but I love him. My whole life I've wished that I was more to him than just a successor. But time is running out, and I can't change who he is any more than he can change me. The same way your mom can't make you want the same things she does."

"I wish it was easier to talk to her. When I'm with you, I'm so much more myself. I don't know how else to explain it."

"I don't get to be myself with many people. And you shouldn't be anything less than yourself with me. I want all of you: the strange, the sweet. You're beautiful to me."

"God, Beau, when you say things like that… How could you possibly know?"

"I don't need to see you to know every part of you is beautiful."

Her beauty shone through her actions, the way she cared for her family, the shows she watched with her dad, the games she played with her nephews. April was a reflection of the deep love she had for the people in her life. The pieces of them she kept and carried forward.

It made Beau want to try harder. To love with the same dedication April did.

"You make me feel beautiful."

"You make me feel…" Where did he even begin? Interesting. Worthy. "Like I might be enough."

It had always been easier to confess into the darkness.

And with April… everything was easier. His feelings

had always run deep. It was his biggest weakness, getting attached quickly.

Even after a month, he could sit and listen to her for hours. The sound of her voice, how she viewed the world with a mix of idealism and passiveness — a strange live and let live but also do better — that he'd never heard acknowledged before.

If only he could condense what he cared for down to a simplicity. Everything he cared about was complicated. His life was complicated. It said something that a disembodied voice was the simplest part of his life.

———

April's namesake brought with it warmer days and a growing need in her heart. Try as she might to sweep it under the rug or cover it up with scrum meetings and pivot tables, the overwhelming joy that filled her every time they spoke was becoming unavoidable.

Beau's candor and charm were addictive. When they talked, she never wanted it to end. But soon, he'd want to meet, and then…

She flipped onto her back, throwing the sheet off her damp skin. The window was cracked open to fight the humidity, but even now, hours after the sun had disappeared, the heat remained. The lazy turning of the ceiling fan did as much as a child blowing out a candle.

Up till now, she had been moving forward, eyes on her future. Each new project she took on, the extra hours she'd put in, the assignments she could have refused — all in aid of the next step.

Now the future looked less certain. She wanted to be with Beau, but how could that work when all of her previous relationships had failed? How many tests would she run before she was broken beyond repair?

"Beau," she whispered into the darkness, hoping. "Are you awake?"

"I'm here."

"Can I tell you a secret?"

"You can tell me everything."

Tonight, every empty space in the room had made itself known. April shuffled closer to the center of the bed, hugging her pillow tight. "I can't stop thinking about you."

"I can't do anything without thinking of you. I even dream of you."

"Why do you think this is happening? Why us?"

"You're as lonely as I am."

April followed the slow rotation of the fan blades, her breathing labored. Of course Beau could tell. Without knowing what she looked like or her full name, he'd seen the emptiness she hid inside.

"April?"

"You're right."

"I know."

"Most people don't see it."

"I'm not most people."

She smiled. "No, you really aren't, are you?"

Maybe no one else could hear the loneliness in his

voice, but it was a potent echo of every night she'd lain in bed, aware of every inch of the empty space beside her.

Flipping her pillow over, she sighed. "I have to meet with the VP tomorrow. Every time I close my eyes, I picture myself ruining it."

"You'll be great. Remember what I said. Everyone in that room has been where you are."

"Awake at two a.m. and talking to the voice in my head?"

His thick, husky laugh rumbled through her mind, spreading electricity to her fingertips.

"I meant standing nervously at the front of the room. We've all been there."

"Even you?"

"Especially me."

April shifted onto her side, hooking her arm under her pillow and pulling it tighter. So tight she could almost hug him. Blinking against the thick darkness in her room, she tried to picture him lying in his bed.

Imagined her fingers tangled in silky strands, stroking the curve of his neck as he whispered to her in the dark.

Soon, he'd want to meet, and she'd have to make a choice. Until then, she'd hold on to the fantasy a little tighter.

"Will you tell me about it?"

Chapter Six

Ruby's apartment always left April feeling unkempt. Her older sister had inherited their mom's height, as well as her veracious organization skills. Spotless surfaces and labels on everything from the pantry to the kids' playroom.

"Dinner is in the fridge. Caleb isn't eating anything green right now, so his is the one with no peas. They should eat by —"

"Seven. Then bath, then bed," April finished. Four years of babysitting her nephews, and her sister still didn't trust her to remember.

"Good." Ruby smoothed out the lines of her dress. The deep green material draped flatteringly across her hips and chest. Ruby had been blessed post pregnancy.

April could only hope to be so lucky.

"Thanks again. I know you don't normally have anything going on, and you know how long it's been since we've had time by ourselves. Besides, the boys love you."

April eyed the living room.

Said boys were being eerily polite, hands in laps, focused on the television.

It was the calm before the storm.

"Of course, it's fine. I'm happy to. I love them too."

Ruby called out to Toby to hurry up, and while her head was turned, the boys shared a mischievous look.

Oh, it was going to be one of those nights.

She followed her sister into the kitchen, biting her tongue when Ruby moved April's bag off the table and tucked it into a wicker storage box in the sideboard.

Everything in its place.

While Ruby called out to Toby to hurry up again, April busied herself with the coffee machine, a black and silver contraption that took up a quarter of their counter space and had a touchscreen. It made more noise than a jackhammer, but it was Toby's pride and joy.

April preferred her pod machine and secretly loved the look on Toby's face every time she mentioned it.

Then she smiled, remembering Beau had shared similar complaints.

Ruby's eyes widened. "You've met someone."

How did she — April schooled her expression. "I haven't —"

But her older sister could sense gossip from a mile away. "Don't even try it. Okay, I need details. Mom doesn't tell me anything."

That was as unbelievable as April's "conversations" with Beau. "Really? She didn't mention the date she set me up on last month?"

"Fine, she did. Wait, please don't tell me you fell in love with the dentist. If you're going to nab a doctor, at least make sure he can get rid of my crow's feet." Ruby pushed back the skin on her temples.

"It's not the dentist. He's…" And damn, how could she describe him? "It's still really new, but he makes me feel…" *Like I'm the only person in the world he'll ever love.*

"Special," she finally said.

Unlike Ruby, who had used her Barbies to act out her crushes on boys in school, April had never chased after love. And before Beau came along, she'd been content with her family and her job.

Last night, Helena had said, "I don't want you to give up on love."

But what had she been giving up, really? A series of short-term relationships and Preston, a guy her mother loved because he'd wanted everything Helena preached. The house, the family…

He just hadn't wanted it with April.

And she hadn't wanted to marry him. If he'd asked, she would have said no. *Not yet. Give me more time.* But he never did, and he'd gotten engaged to Melody before the end of the year. They were pregnant with their second kid, last April heard.

It shouldn't hurt. She had everything she wanted — her family, her career…

And Beau, for now.

When he was a child, there was always someone, multiple someone's — nannies, tutors, then girlfriends, journalists — hovering over Beau's shoulder, scrutinizing his choices, criticizing his every move. *Not like that. Do better.*

He'd quickly grown sick of attention. The kind he'd grown up with, the kind he'd grown used to, wasn't about him. No one really looked. They would only watch and comment and project. He was the vision board they pinned their dreams on.

Fundraisers like today were part of the package deal he'd inherited as JP junior. After ducking out of at least three conversations regarding his father's absence and one slimy pitch for backdoor campaign donations that made Beau want to immediately take a shower, he had situated himself on the outskirts of the ballroom, hiding in plain sight.

The event was being held in the private space above a local art gallery in a blatant attempt to appeal to the community. But the four-hundred-dollar bottles of champagne spoke to the true nature of those in attendance. All around him were the usual suspects — business owners, CEOs, board members, local politicians, and a handful of football players who'd earn an appearance fee for *lending their support*. A sea of designer labels and plastered on smiles concealed for-profit conversations. It left Beau nauseous. It was everything he hated about his role as a Forrester.

"The prodigal son in the flesh. I seem to remember you saying you hated all this pompous bullshit. But I guess your old man can't keep saving your ass forever."

Beau's teeth ached as he ground them together. Mason fucking Hedges, crypto currency douche and the only man he knew who would eagerly campaign for asshole of the year.

Mason was the poster child for arrogant dicks everywhere. Since school, he'd been a thorn in Beau's side, always finding opportunities to suck the joy out of a room while simultaneously filling it with his own sense of superiority. It left the taste of bile in Beau's throat every time.

"Mason."

"Oh, don't be like that. We're practically partners."

JP, in all his wisdom, had been a major investor when Mason's company went public. It didn't make them anything close to partners, but it did give Mason the opportunity to annoy the shit out of Beau.

He'd wipe that smile off his face soon enough. When Beau took over, those shares would be sold, and he didn't care to whom. The massive dump would no doubt result in a selling frenzy.

Beau couldn't wait.

Mason slithered closer. "Surprised the old man isn't here. There must be some truth to the rumors."

"He had other obligations. Pity you didn't."

"And miss seeing the golden boy fumbling? Never. Daddy should have done a better job training you."

Honestly, if JP were here, he'd likely agree.

"Mason, if you spent more time paying attention and less time patting yourself on the back with your soul-sucking podcast buddies, you'd know not to antagonize someone who owns a majority share of your company."

"Oh, I love it when you talk dirty."

Beau held back his laughter, then decided, fuck it, he didn't care what Mason thought.

The asshole smirked. "If the day ever comes that JP trusts you to take over, I'm going to watch gleefully while you drive his legacy into the ground."

Fire surged through Beau's throat, and he walked away before it manifested into something he couldn't take back. Fuck Mason and his pointy chin. He'd always known which buttons to push.

It was Beau's own fault. Years ago, he'd made the mistake of thinking Mason would understand — another single son shouldering his father's reputation. Instead, Mason had taken every chance he could to remind Beau of his misplaced trust and highlight the exact reason Beau's choices were moot. Whether Beau stayed or left, the result was likely the same.

Total destruction.

He signaled the bartender. "Bourbon, neat, biggest glass you've got."

"Wow, you're either having the best day or the worst."

"Worst," he said. "I'm stuck at a fundraiser, and the one person I was avoiding found me. But my night just got better."

"Who's the dick?"

"Mason Hedges. He's the poster boy for 'effective altruism.'"

"I can hear those air quotes," she laughed. *"Wait. He calls himself that?"*

Beau swallowed a laugh, feigning interest in a Klimt as he took a sip of bourbon. "And more. I don't like to think badly of people, but he is easily the worst person I've ever met."

It should be legal to punch someone that vile.

There were a few lonely community members scattered here tonight — the only people Beau could stomach at these events — but the rest lived to make Beau question his commitment to a clean record.

"I haven't even met him, and I agree with you. And I'm more than happy to think badly of people for the both of us."

"I see Mason got to you too."

Beau huffed a laugh before turning to Bonnie.

"Hi, Bonnie," he said for April's benefit. "My first order of business will be to blacklist him from any building I enter."

Making Bonnie laugh on purpose was a new experience. Any other time she'd laughed in his presence, he'd suspected it was at his expense.

"I almost didn't come tonight for the risk of seeing him. But it was my only chance to talk to the mayor about how we might reduce the delays on the airport link."

He'd heard about the project, of course, but Forrester wasn't involved. And the proposed rail upgrades were said to be so expensive that even state government officials were cautious to give an expected delivery of fewer than ten years. Did Bonnie know something he didn't?

"You want to back the connected rail project?"

"Bonnie better say yes. That project will be a lifesaver for anyone living in the eastern suburbs. Better yet, ask if she wants to run your company for you."

Beau stilled.

She was joking, but… she wasn't wrong.

———

April threw herself onto the couch, her muscles aching, and drank in the peaceful quiet. Getting the boys to bed was an extreme sport.

She loved her nephews, but… her sister deserved a medal. How had her parents raised four of them?

Beau wanted kids. More than one, he'd said, because he'd always wanted a brother or sister growing up. He'd be a great dad. April could already see him in the kitchen, teaching them to cook. He'd make animals out of pancake batter, and he'd taste like sugar and sunshine.

Her heart aching wildly, April closed her eyes and took a deep breath.

She still wasn't sure she wanted children. Had she daydreamed about it? Sure. A tiny hand in hers as they walked the markets, perhaps a little girl who would look at her with brown hair and a button nose.

It was a lovely dream and a dangerous hope.

Before Beau, she hadn't realized it was possible to fall for someone she'd never met. Sure, she'd heard stories — people who started out as pen pals or long-distance matches on apps — but she'd never *known*, not really.

And yet... here she was, hook, line, and sinkered to Beau's compassion, humor, and his unending sweetness.

Chapter Seven

The leather chair groaned as he dropped into it.

JP had obviously noticed how often he hid in Keaton's old office — he'd taken to dropping by Beau's side of the eighty-fifth floor unannounced and texting (something Beau hadn't even known his father *could* do) when Beau wasn't there.

And yet, strangely, JP hadn't demanded an explanation.

Across the street, the building was dark. It seemed even the workaholic redhead next door had more of a life than he did.

If only he could stop wanting the life he couldn't have. It was a lost cause. Thirty-three years. Surely, he should have given up on that hope by now.

He wanted to be a man who could make his own decisions, live his own life. No matter how unpalatable those decisions were to his father.

All day, his chest had grown tight under the weight

of his dilemma. Slowly squeezing until it was difficult to take a full breath. Meeting after meeting, he'd pushed through, ignoring the cramp.

Now, in the solace of an empty building, he loosened his tie and forced the air into his lungs, holding it until it hurt.

One, two, three, four, five.

He didn't want this. But what other choice did he have?

What he wouldn't give for a simpler life. To walk away from his father and toward the only person who saw him. The only one he wanted.

With every conversation, his resolve slipped. He longed for her to know him, to choose him.

If he knew it wouldn't scare April off, he'd have asked for her number, whisked her off to try the chef's selection at *Pour Toujour*, where they could eat with their hands and she'd no doubt drive him crazy with every lick of her fingers.

Would she let him send her flowers? Maybe he could buy tickets to the run of *Swan Lake* they were sponsoring. Did she like ballet? Or there was a twilight concert next month, Poppy someone, would she want to see that? He could leave VIP tickets by the door so she could pick them up. Or...

"Oh."

One small word stole Beau's breath.

Despite having never heard it before, there was no mistaking it.

"April?"

Silence. Then, *"Beau? Shit. I was just, um…"*

"Am I interrupting something?"

"Kind of. I'm in the shower."

Christ. They hadn't faced this situation before. The closest they'd come had been when Beau was getting ready at the gym. But there was something else, a breathiness in April's voice that spiked Beau's arousal.

"It's late. Do you always shower at night?"

"Yeah. I used to take long showers when I was younger. As many as I could. It was the only way I could be alone."

"How was your dad about that?"

She laughed. *"Mad at first. Used to complain about the bills. But I negotiated with him."*

Adorable. He could imagine April, her list of pros and cons, making her case. Fuck. He wished he could kiss her. "What was the compromise?"

"I was allowed twenty minutes, as long as I made sure I waited for everyone else first. It's actually why I'm such a night owl now. Waiting for everyone else to get out, then for the hot water to return. Some nights, it was after eleven before I had my turn."

He chuckled. "Was it worth it?"

"Definitely," she said, and Jesus, was it just him or did her voice get thicker? Was she…? *"I was a very horny teenager."*

"Fuck," he said, palming himself.

"Did you ever…?"

He was hard as nails, his dick thick along his thigh, trapped in his tailored pants. A wet spot from his precum cooling against his heated skin already.

It wouldn't take much to send him over the edge,

knowing April was in the shower right now, naked, wet, reminiscing about illicit orgasms. He squeezed the base of his cock, trying to stem the blood flow, give himself more time.

"Anywhere and everywhere I could."

Her response was a breathy laugh that trailed off into a low moan. Shit. Was she?

Their connection usually only carried over what was said aloud, but right now, Beau could hear every sound she was making, down her stuttered, panting breaths.

She was touching herself.

He wanted to get himself off. Everyone had gone home for the night, including JP, and the door to his office was locked.

"Usually, I'm in bed when I do this, but I was thinking about you, and I couldn't help myself."

Fuck it.

Beau made short work of unzipping his pants and pulling himself out.

"Describe what you're doing," he said. "I want to see you."

"I'm," she started, followed by a shallow moan, *"I'm lying in the tub, and I'm using the showerhead to —"*

"Is it a handheld?"

"Yes."

He groaned.

"I've got the, oh, the water falling on my…" She paused.

"Your pussy." She was glistening, wet and open. Fuck, he could see it. "Is it hitting your clit?"

"Yes," she moaned, and the sound of it made him impossibly hard.

Beau closed his eyes and wrapped his hand around his cock, stroking with a growing speed. He twisted his fist at the tip, squeezing the head and coating his palm with precum, growing slicker with each pass. He spread his knees wide, fucking up into his hand, imagining the way her juices would coat him.

"What are you thinking about?"

"You. Your hands. Your mouth."

Dropping his other hand to his chest, he pinched his nipple through his shirt. It would be better if he took it off, but stopping was out of the question.

His voice came out a thick rasp. "If I were there, I wouldn't be able to keep my mouth off you. I'd kiss down your neck, between your breasts, trace the under-side with my tongue."

April moaned. Maybe the connection was stronger in this moment, but each sound she made pressed against every corner of Beau's mind, slipping down his spine, a straight shot to his cock.

"I bet you taste incredible." He closed his eyes. "God, I want to taste you. I want to bury myself between your legs, open you up with my mouth." He sped up his strokes. "You're soaking."

"Beau..."

Fuck.

"Please."

His fist was a blur over his cock. "What do you want?"

"I want you to fuck me," she whispered.

Her panted whines were driving him crazy. The breathy gasps she let out as she touched herself ignited something hot in his gut, and he moaned. *Fuck,* he wanted that too. He'd make sure there was no room for her to think about anything else. Just his touch, his lips, his cock.

"Use your fingers. Imagine I'm there with you. Open up for me." A groan escaped at the sounds she made, gasps between syllables, loose and mindless. "Feel how hot and wet you are. God, you're amazing. I want you to fuck yourself with your fingers, in and out, just the way you need it."

"Oh my god."

"Keep going. Tell me how it feels."

"So... good. Beau..."

His strokes came firmer, faster. He could picture her, splayed open, so sexy. He gripped himself tighter. The leather chair groaned in time with his thrusts, warm precum slicking every movement, until he could almost feel himself buried within her dripping pussy.

"Please."

Fuck. She was going to kill him. Dead before he'd get the chance to hear her laugh in person. Before he could kiss her.

"Are you close?"

"Yes. So close..."

His own climax built, his muscles tensing as he fucked up into his fist, his hand a blur over the head. Pleasure burned in his chest, his thighs, all the way down to his toes. He slid his free hand into his hair, needing to grip something, anything, in the absence of her.

"You feel incredible — hot and tight around me. Are you going to come thinking of me inside you? Fucking you?"

"Yes, *please.*"

He was close. He could feel it, barely held at bay, slowing his hand to wait it out because he needed to hear her. Needed to have his wits about himself so he could take in every detail. She was fucking exquisite. A masterpiece. A treasure.

Oh, if she were here, he'd sacrifice himself upon her altar, follow through on every single word.

He'd make sure of it. Given the chance, he'd take care of her in every way she let him. Fulfilling her needs while she was busy looking after everyone else. And he'd do it so well, she'd never want anyone else.

"Do it. Let me hear you."

"Beau."

"That's it. Come for me."

"Oh god…"

Then the sweetest sound of all passed her lips. His name had never sounded better. It was drawn out, becoming two syllables when a moan broke through, and he was fucking done for.

His orgasm ripped through him, her voice ringing in his ears as he grunted and came over his fist. The sound echoed in the quiet of the room, and for a single moment, it was as if she were there.

Beau dropped his hand to his hip and stared up at

the ceiling, panting loudly. His heart pounded so hard he was practically vibrating.

He was damp with sweat, sticky on his stomach, trying to regain his composure. The image of her was burned into his retinas, skin soaked and legs trembling. What had she looked like when she came? Did she blush? Head thrown back, mouth opened wide? Did she close her eyes?

For all intents and purposes, they'd just fucked. The fact of it thickened the air.

"I wish you were here."

There was a gaping chasm in his heart the shape and breadth of her.

But she deserved more than a man who was scared to take his own future into his hands.

It was time to step up and hope that when the time came, he'd done enough.

Chapter Eight

Beau had grown up with plenty of *residences* — being a Forrester meant owning a piece of land in almost every landmark city — but he had never had a *home*.

JP wouldn't understand the difference. Why would he? Home to him was the company. It had taken Beau a long time to stop asking why his father loved the city more than he loved his son.

How ironic that he had then fallen for it himself.

But Chance was so much more than Beau had expected. The heart of the city was in its people, the millions of stories collectively being told in real time. He'd seen glimpses of it, pockets of people gravitating together — grad students on the west side, older families to the south. They protected and supported each other.

Fundraisers, protests, volunteering. Food drives and marathons and free concerts in the park.

He should have resented the city, but he didn't. He cared deeply about Chance, and he wouldn't want to live anywhere else. But he still longed for someone to call home.

This mass of glass and steel might be his father's sanctuary, but it had only ever served as Beau's cage.

Every article on JP called him a corporate savant, but when it came to his son, JP was willfully ignorant. Jesus. Even Mason fucking Hedges knew Beau wasn't the man for the job.

Far better to find someone who was. Let them take the company into the next generation. Beau would happily shift his focus to funding community projects.

Not that he had the spare time to enjoy them himself.

"I'll sleep when I retire," he had said to April this morning. It was becoming increasingly common to find her awake at one a.m. He'd worry more if he wasn't so damn happy to talk to her.

"Is that what your dad has done?" she had asked.

Oh, she had his number.

The truth was, if he followed in JP's footsteps, he'd never retire. He'd simply work until he couldn't anymore.

Had he even earned it?

He'd been born a Forrester. No skill required.

What could he possibly offer April — capable, sexy April — who worked her ass off every day, except a life of postponed promises?

Waiting for him to come home, waiting for him to retire.

No amount of money or power could compete with her tenacity. If he wanted her, he had to do better. He needed to deserve her.

Dedicating himself to someone? Now *that* would be a worthy cause.

With that in mind, he straightened his shoulders and walked into Bonnie's office. The succession announcement would be made in three weeks, so they had a lot of work ahead of them.

He hoped Bonnie was willing to hear him out.

———

If she'd thought it was difficult to concentrate before, it was far worse now. Now that she knew exactly how Beau sounded when he came.

She'd once caught him mid-run, his voice husky and breathy and the purest embodiment of the phrase panty-melting. It wasn't as if April had *deliberately* imagined what his sex voice sounded like before last week, but now that she had heard it for real, it was playing on repeat in her brain.

Getting through her work had never been harder.

It wasn't limited to sex either.

April had told him things she hadn't admitted to anyone. It was easier in the quiet of her bedroom, without the fear of him seeing her, to crack open her chest of secrets. Lay herself before him.

And he'd bared himself to her.

Was falling for him more or less absurd than the phenomenon that let them talk to each other?

She couldn't even claim it had happened without her noticing, because she'd been there. For every conversation and laugh. One amazing orgasm.

And it was clear he felt the same, but he still hadn't suggested they meet. April wasn't ready for that anyway, except…

Why hadn't he asked?

The more she analyzed the possibilities, the less she liked them.

After the third error popped up, April gave up. She needed a break.

This was ridiculous. She had two degrees. Had saved the company millions of dollars with recommendations based on her insights. She didn't need the validation of a man to prove her worth.

So it was stupid to be scared of him.

If he didn't want to meet her, that was his problem. In fact, the longer she thought about it, the more she realized she didn't want to meet him. Why ruin a perfectly fine… whatever it is they were, by trying to turn it into something it wasn't? Sometimes the data didn't support the result she wanted, and that was okay. If Beau only liked her because she was still the idea of a person and not the messy, awkward reality, then she'd have to accept that.

If the man of her dreams didn't want her, she'd

simply cut herself off from dating and live a life of quiet devastation.

No big deal.

One thing was certain — the spreadsheet in front of her wouldn't offer any solutions. Sighing, she pushed back from her desk, spinning in her chair and checking in on the office across the street.

Data was something most misunderstood. What looked simple — rows and rows of answers, black and white, stretching out with no delicacy — held untold secrets, if you knew where to look. It was all in the asking.

April likened it to a magician's trick. Analytics was all about looking right while everyone else looked left.

The office across the way was empty again. It stayed empty for hours at a time, and then spontaneously, the same man, pressed and polished (and gorgeous), would appear.

Sometimes, she'd spot him on the train ride home. He never looked anything less than refined, his small smile calling to her like a locked door. Part of her still wanted to talk to him, say *something*, but she never did.

People had never been as straightforward as numbers were.

So she sat in silence and wondered.

———

Bonnie had said *yes*. Granted, he'd have to announce it to his father and get the paperwork in order before the thirtieth, which would be a tall order. Especially if JP fired him for insubordination.

Beau wouldn't put it past him. Keep the job and live on to a hundred just to spite everyone, despite every doctor in the country telling him he'd be lucky to see twelve months.

But, even with the fear that his father might find a way to legally bind him to the role, Beau felt lighter. Today he'd made a choice, a step toward the future he wanted.

And he couldn't have done it without April.

"You're falling for a *voice in your head*?"

It didn't sound any less ridiculous when Keaton said it.

"Her name is April."

"Her name is probably Earl. Haven't you ever heard of the term catfish?"

"Fuck you," Beau said, laughing.

Sure, the thought had crossed Beau's mind. In the beginning. But they knew each other now. They'd shared intimate details of their lives.

"I've heard her voice —"

"Oh wait, I think the past is calling. It wants its outdated gender norms back."

Beau shook his head. "Come on Keats, I trust her."

"Well, shit. I can't remember the last time you said that. You really do like her." Keaton blew out a long breath. "And she has no idea who you are?"

Finally, the problem.

"No."

"You know that's going to be a problem, don't you? Either she thinks you've been lying to her this whole time, or you freak her out with the whole 'hey, I'm secretly a billionaire' thing."

Beau hung his head. "Why do you think I called you?"

Chapter Nine

April covered her yawn with a hand. All she wanted was to head home, crawl under her sheets, and sleep. Last night, she'd had an epiphany regarding the migration of their data lake files, and then Beau had been awake, so they'd spent an hour swapping embarrassing drunken stories from college.

Collecting Helena's order at the butcher at daybreak on a Sunday after five hours of broken sleep wasn't her idea of fun, but she'd promised.

"Number thirty-eight!"

April stepped up to the counter. "Morning, Sal."

Sal's presence in Southport had been larger than life for over thirty years. A longtime family friend, he'd once been in the running for her grandmother's hand — a story he told regularly, and which changed every time. April had a soft spot for the old guy.

Even though his shoulders barely cleared the high counter, there was nothing small about him. His eyes lit up. "Ah, the enigmatic April Swan! You look beautiful, as always. How is your mother?"

His joy was contagious, even at seven a.m. "She's well. Sent me here for her usual if you have it."

Sal tipped his head. "Of course I do. I always keep some haddock aside for her. Let me head into the back. I'll wrap it up special."

"Thanks, Sal."

"Who's Sal, and why are you thanking him this early in the morning? Do I need to straighten him out?"

The shop gleamed in the morning light — clean, white surfaces packed with various meats. Sal's Shop — aptly and lazily named — had been a stalwart for as long as April could remember.

"He's our butcher," she whispered, pretending to study cuts of ox tail. "There's only one man I want."

"I dreamed of you last night."

April's heart sped up.

"We were at my house along the coast. You'd love it. There are endless beach views, showers we can both fit into —"

She ducked her head, hoping to hide the blush on her cheeks.

"— and a fire pit for when the temperature drops. You'd sneak a look at your emails while I slept in, and then I'd distract you with my mouth until nothing and no one mattered but me. And then we'd lay around, and I'd just hold you."

Words had left her. "Beau…"

"Here you go, April," Sal said, returning. The wrinkles in his brow deepened with concern. "Are you all right?"

There was no easy answer. If meeting Beau had been like the beginnings of a rollercoaster, every conversation now felt like the last loop. The platform was approaching, and she'd have to decide whether she was getting off.

There was never enough time.

April paid and tossed the change into his tip jar. "I hope so."

———

Ever since her disastrous date with Dylan, an idea had been tap-tap-tapping at the corners of her mind. A possible way to bring Beau closer, without crossing the unspoken boundary they had in place.

Tests were an important part of the development phase, after all. It wasn't possible to prove a theory without them, and if this worked, then maybe they could put off meeting a little longer. Just… until she could be certain.

The Southport markets on a Sunday were a flurry of activity, and even before April caught the scent of coffee, cinnamon, and bacon, a series of familiar faces called morning greetings as she passed.

Decades of Sundays had been spent here, setting up pottery with her mom, laying out prices and herding people toward the tent. Barely a weekend of her childhood had passed without being here, Liam and Ruby always sticking close to Helena, Eli hiding in the back, and April merrily running errands, using each opportunity to explore every square inch of the marketplace.

"Morning, dear. Are you here to help your mom?" Mrs. Peterson asked, filling a bowl with handmade soaps.

"Just picking up Felix today."

"That's lovely. Make sure you come by and say hello. I've got a new one with Manuka honey and pomegranate."

"Sure thing."

Rows and rows of stalls were coming together, a good chunk of the owners waving to April as she made her way to the back corner. Half of the area was reserved for goods, and the other half delegated to food — fresh produce and the more recent addition of food trucks. The air was thick with memories, blasting open the bay windows in April's mind and whisking her through a montage of her formative years.

Perfect.

She knew exactly what her first date with Beau would be.

———

Beau ladled soup into a bowl, breathing in the rich, salty smell. "Ready to eat?"

"Thank god. I was about to starve."

"Patience is a virtue."

Cooking had always been therapeutic. He'd had a

lot of spare time growing up, and being directly involved in every step of the process was immensely satisfying.

Of course, he hadn't realized how hard teaching April would be when he couldn't show her anything. But she'd vetoed a video call, and so he did the best she could.

"Say that to my stomach."

What he would give to make that promise a reality. "I'll be sure to pass it along the next time I see it."

After adding the extremely crispy bacon (*"I won't eat flaccid bacon,"* April had emphatically stated, and he would now forever be aroused by breakfast meat), they sat to eat.

"Oh my god, this soup is amazing."

"Thank you." It was good, and hopefully, the first of many meals they'd share together.

"What happened next?"

"Dad kicked up a fuss, made the cab driver sign a waiver, and made a generous donation to the college, after which I was offered the opportunity to retake the exam and an apology for their mix-up."

"Their mix-up?"

The soup was cheesy and salty and delicious. "That's JP for you. I did everything I could to skip that final, and he still managed to get the upper hand."

"Unbelievable."

"You've got that right."

"He should get together with my mother. Together they could teach a masterclass on how to meddle."

"Have you talked to her about it? She might surprise you if you ask her to stop setting you up."

"Have you told your dad that you don't want to be CEO?"

"You know I haven't."

"Do you think he'll think less of you?"

He set his spoon down. "My father has never thought much of me."

"And what do you think?"

The scrape of the bowl echoed as he pushed it away. Talk of JP always ruined his appetite.

"What if I've wasted my chance to do something meaningful?"

"Even if that was true — which it isn't — do you really believe you couldn't make a change now?"

As if it were that easy. Beau smiled into the emptiness of his room. "You make it sound so simple."

"Don't you want to be happy?"

Happiness…. What a foreign concept. Contentment had always been all Beau could hope for. A balance between his duty and his will.

Until recently.

"You make me happy."

———

Moonlight streaked across his room; the full moon determined not to let Beau hide away tonight. It was awful, not seeing April in these moments, when time stretched out and the distance between them grew. Being unable to touch her left a physical ache, one that had settled under his rib cage and refused to budge.

"Can I tell you a secret?"

"You can tell me anything."

"I never used to keep pillows on the left side of my bed. But now I do. On nights when I can't sleep," she admitted, her voice hushed, *"I'll roll over so I can cuddle into them, imagining it's you."*

Beau clenched his bedsheets in his fists.

"I used to take a walk when I got stressed at work." She continued before he could respond. *"But lately I listen to music instead."*

"Anything I'd know?"

"They're too obscure for you."

Beau laughed. He was so doomed. No one would ever compare now.

"I never had photos in my apartment before we met. I didn't understand why anyone would want so many eyes following them around when all I've ever wanted was to be left alone. But hearing you talk about your family has made me notice how unconnected I've been from my own life. I've been existing, but you make me want to live."

His next thought caught in his throat. This was always his problem. The feelings loomed large in his chest, not fully formed, barely ever visited, even in his most private moments. As if to think them, acknowledge them, was too much. He forced himself now. If he couldn't tell April, he'd never tell anyone, and that in itself would mean he was giving up, wouldn't it?

"I've spent my whole life afraid that I would never find love. How would I even recognize it? I sure as hell never got it from JP. And when your own father can't love you…"

The air felt thick and heavy in his chest, a veritable storm cloud rolling against his rib cage.

"What if I'm chasing a fantasy?" he asked to his ceiling, a sharp huff of pained laughter echoing in his mind. A fantasy, indeed. Look who he was talking to. Someone, somewhere, was laughing at him, he'd put money on it.

"*Beau*," and oh, the emotions April could incite with a single syllable.

He rubbed his sternum, trying to dislodge the ache. "I wish I didn't want it so badly, but I do. I can't stop wanting it."

"Don't you ever feel like you're going to burst? Holding all of that inside?"

"All the fucking time. But what other option do I have? Walk away?"

"Why not?"

"Said someone whose parents wouldn't disown them. You have no idea what my life is like."

"You're right. But that doesn't make me wrong."

He hated it when sense rained on his parade. It always sounded so much like JP.

"You're choosing to be miserable. You might not like the alternative, but you can't blame anyone else for your choice."

He sat up, the stark wall cold against his bare back, his gut churning. The anger had nowhere to go but out.

"And what about you? Because from where I stand, there doesn't seem to be a downside to your situation. You don't want to get married right away? So what? You still want a relationship. Your mom might not under-stand the idea of not having kids, but she'll still be there for you. You're lucky she cares enough to badger you about it. I think you're worried she'll stop if you tell her."

"And you aren't? I never took you for a hypocrite, Beau. Tell me the truth. Why are you so afraid of him?"

Beau dug his hands into his hair, pulling roughly. Maybe he was doomed to be a disappointment. To April and his father. To everyone.

"And what happens if I leave and it kills him? Regardless of what happened in the past, I don't want that on my conscience."

"All the more reason for you to be honest. You don't have much time with him. He should know the real you."

The real him… Beau wasn't sure who that even was. Was he the responsible son? The lonely bachelor? The pining hero? Who was he to April?

"You know how much I want that. At least your mother loves you, even if she pushes."

"Then why can't she trust me when I tell her I'm happy? It's as if what I want doesn't matter. I love her, but I want something different from her life."

The emptiness enveloped him in its long arms, squeezing out the last of his anger with a final sigh.

"You want to make your own choices, and your own mistakes. Not to retrace someone else's steps."

"Yes."

They were two sides of the same coin. *Perfectly matched.*

"I wish I knew how to talk to him."

"You can talk to me."

"You're different. I wake up wanting to talk to you. I fall asleep dreaming of you. I can't remember my life before you, and I don't want a future without you."

The silence bled out, merging seamlessly into the shadows.

"You shouldn't be so afraid of being her, you know," he said when it became clear April wasn't going to speak. "Of wanting those things. Making the same choices doesn't mean having the same regrets."

"I know," she murmured. *"And I know it doesn't make sense. But that doesn't make it any easier. See, this is why I avoid emotions."*

"You can't avoid them forever. What happens when you fall in love?"

It was quiet for so long, Beau wondered if April hadn't shut him out completely. *Still too needy.* Maybe he shouldn't have hoped, but this ride only had one destination for him. He wanted April by his side for it.

"Love is for the brave. Or at least people braver than me."

What bullshit. He wanted to rip the hinges off his door and *prove* to her how wrong she was. "You're not a coward." If anyone was, it was him. "You love your family, and you want to make them happy. But you can't forget your own happiness in the process."

As if he could talk. He was worse than a coward; he

was a fraud. He might have set things in motion with Bonnie, but he was no closer to telling JP about their plans, nor telling April the truth about himself.

"What if she's right? What if I'm making the wrong choice, and by the time I have it figured out, it's too late?"

He'd wondered the same thing almost every night. The only part of his life he didn't question was April.

Bad choices did exist, and there was such a thing as too late. His life was a testament to that. But Beau lived in a world of compromise. April deserved better.

———

There was a strange weightlessness to being up all night — a sense of being part of her own dreams.

Dreams that now included Beau.

"Why can't you have both?"

There was April's deepest secret. She wanted it all, but she couldn't take the next step. "I'm not saying I can't, it's just… I'm not ready yet."

There were still tests she hadn't run, data she didn't have. She wasn't about to risk her heart with a hasty decision.

"Can I ask you something?"

She twisted the rings on her right hand. "Of course."

"At what point will you feel you've achieved what you're working toward? Because I've seen what making work your life can do, and if you don't make room for the other parts of yourself — passion, care, family — you'll forget how."

April closed her eyes, heat prickling the corners. In the last few years — pretty much since Preston had left — work had been her escape, filling in the gaps of her loneliness with the one part of her life she had control over.

"I know you want to fix the problems no one else can. But that doesn't have to mean passing up everything else. Wouldn't love be the ultimate mystery to solve?"

Damn him. "It's not fair for you to say these things and be so far away. How am I supposed to kiss you?"

"You can owe me one. I'll start a tab for you."

Her laughter pushed a tear from her eye. It wasn't fair. Beau was everything she wanted. And it terrified her.

Of all the miracles in all the world, why did Beau have to appear now?

The platform was close now. The space between them felt thick, sticky with anticipation.

How cruel to make her choose. She was already attached, sweetly addicted to his conversation and company. Even when they talked, she missed him. And he wanted more. She could hear it in his voice, the hints at meeting, of making this real. Tangible. Forever.

She wavered the most at night, when his silky rich tones wrapped around her like a blanket, holding her in the darkness. It would be so easy to say yes. Swap numbers, arrange to meet.

Then she woke up, and the harsh reality of her life reminded her why. Why she couldn't. Not even for Beau, a man even her own mother wouldn't find fault with.

Someone Helena would have built in a lab if she'd known how.

Could reality ever live up to the fantasy of Beau she'd been dreaming of?

Or would meeting shatter it all?

Chapter Ten

When April had dictated a web address to him, Beau could admit to being worried. He'd expected to be caught in his omissions, maybe finding an exposé on him or his father, or the Top 40 under 40 list he'd been in last August.

Instead, there was an address and a map of a local market on the outskirts of the city, complete with a series of numbered dots with attached voice files.

It was the single most romantic thing anyone had ever done for him.

"When I suggested sending you a gift, you refused, but you've created a whole app —"

"Please. It's a couple of voice files. I'm an analyst, not a developer. And that gift" — Beau smiled at the way her voice rose. It always hitched a little higher when she was really worked up — *"cost over four hundred dollars."*

"And?" He would find a way to give it to her. Eventually.

"Just tell me when you get there."

The train uptown ran less frequently on Sunday mornings, but Beau enjoyed the quiet, soaking up the glittering sunlight as they crossed the river into the city. Green dotted every nook and cranny of the skyline now, the riverside blooming with color. On the other side of the bridge, the foot traffic grew denser, runners and cyclists taking advantage of the early spring light.

He really did love this city.

It was a short walk from the terminal, although unfamiliar. Despite traversing the city as often as he could, he hadn't come this far since he was a kid, and he couldn't quite remember why.

He pulled up the map as he approached.

"I'm here."

"Okay," she said, her voice shaky. *"Follow the exact path I've outlined in blue, and each time you reach a green dot, stop and click on it. I've recorded a message at each one."*

Beau admired the handiwork of the map April had retrofitted together in — as she modestly put it — no time at all. He desperately wanted to wrap his arms around her and never let her leave. He was head over heels, and the feeling grew with every breath. At this rate, he'd have a ring by next week.

"Why not walk me through yourself?" He didn't want to say goodbye yet. He never did.

"I never know how long we'll be able to talk for, and I…" The breathiness of her voice cascaded over him, a shiver following in its path despite the morning's increasing warmth. *"This way you have something of me to keep."*

His heart had never stood a chance.

"How do I know you aren't secretly watching me?"

"Because you trust me," she said. He could listen to her read the phone book. An economic report. Tax reform. Whatever it took to never be without the sound.

Her compassion.

Her.

"I wish I could see you."

"You'll have to use your imagination."

The markets were a sight, stalls assembled like an urban maze, utilizing every spare inch of space. And it was *busy*. Busier than Beau had expected.

People moved slower. Kids and dogs and laughter mingled with the heavy smells of bread and fish and meat. Vendors had conversations across the aisle, families stopped to greet old friends. There was organic dog food, florists, handmade cutting blocks, play dough, a dog wash, a gin tasting, and a large seating area where a single man and a guitar had drawn a crowd. Beau watched as the musician invited some of the kids up to help him, giving them shakers and other instruments to play with.

Beau swallowed hard.

It was beautiful.

Finding a community within the office blocks and hotels wasn't easy, but here it was. A little corner of Chance, thriving under the combined love and affection of its citizens.

His chest heaved as he took a deep breath. How had he missed this?

He popped in his ear buds and tapped the first number.

April's voice spilled out, warm and effusive, as he arrived at a berry stand. She was bright, like spring blossoms and cool water. In that moment, absorbing her words, he felt awake, alive, ready for anything. As if a veil had been lifted, the saturation on the world turned up.

"When I was seven, I was convinced that blueberries would turn me into that girl from Willy Wonka, *and I staged a mission to rid the world of them. I even recruited my brother, Eli, who would act as the distraction while I hid the berries. I didn't actually have a plan, so my mom found me trying to stuff them into her purse. Pam, who ran the berry stall, thought it was hilarious. My mom definitely didn't. I was grounded for a month. I still can't eat them."*

———

By the end of the tour, Beau had consumed more cheese than anyone should, a vegan honey he wasn't sure he wanted to know the ingredients of, and a peppermint gin so good he'd bought two.

Every single stop had included a story, a little piece of April's history, but also the history of the markets themselves. She'd obviously come here a lot — since birth from the sounds of it — and Beau was shocked to discover a lot of the people she'd mentioned still working there. At one point, while buying a scented candle, he had spotted a familiar flash of auburn hair and found his mysterious neighbor on the opposite side of the markets.

By the time he'd next looked, she was gone.

As he approached a pottery stand, one of the few stalls not mentioned on his tour, he was even more certain of how he felt about April.

"You look like you're having a good morning."

Beau smiled at the owner, an older woman with short white hair and an assessing gaze.

"I'm having a great morning."

He gravitated toward a small sculpture of a fox.

"Do you like pottery?"

"I like animals."

He tried not to fidget while she looked him over. With a stare like that, she could give JP a run for his money.

With a hum, she reached behind her and produced a pair of swans in black and white, beaks touching in a kiss.

Beau handled it carefully.

"You like it," she said, sure.

"I do." He handed over cash. "Did you know that while swans have been used as a symbol of everlasting love, the males frequently cheat?"

"How depressing. I have a pair of otters holding hands if you'd like to ruin those too."

Beau opened his mouth, ready to apologize, only to find a sly grin on her face. Somehow, it reminded him of April.

She handed him a card. *Helena's Handcrafts.*

"Are you Helena?" he asked.

She nodded.

He held out a hand. "Beau Forrester. Nice to meet you."

If she knew who he was, it didn't show. "You too." Helena wrapped the swans in tissue. "If anything else catches your eye, you might want to get it now before the markets close for good. There's almost a hundred years of history here, and the city would rather have another apartment building than keep it."

He tucked the swans into his pocket, careful to protect them.

"I'll keep that in mind," he said.

She gave him another assessment. "You aren't single, are you? Because I have a daughter about your age," Helena said.

Maybe he would have said yes a few months ago. His gut instinct could usually be trusted, and he liked Helena. Any daughter of hers would likely be worth meeting. But he only wanted April.

"I'm flattered, but I'm seeing someone, and it would be difficult to find anyone better."

"She's a lucky woman."

"I'm the one who's lucky, believe me."

———

The pair of swans took pride of place on his nightstand. It amplified the stark emptiness of his apartment.

He wished she'd been there today, in person. Could

imagine holding her close, his claim staked for everyone to see. They'd make new memories — at the markets, by the river, in her bed.

If she'd asked him to meet her, he would have said yes.

He'd followed orders his whole life, but he was ready to finally take his first steps. Being a Forrester had shown him the value of conviction. Don't simply take action. Charge wholeheartedly forward.

All or nothing.

And he chose *all*.

Chapter Eleven

Technically, Beau had already done the hard part. Getting Bonnie on board and officiating the change behind the scenes had taken weeks. They'd had to be extremely careful. Any slip-ups, and the cat would have sprinted out of the bag faster than Mason could say "non-fungible token."

Beau had hoped to avoid this. Confrontations with JP rarely went well, and the last time Beau had disagreed with him, they hadn't talked for two years.

But JP didn't have two years, and Beau didn't want a fight to be the last memory he had of his father. Whatever happened, they were still family.

April had reassured him last night. Calmed him with terrible dad jokes, and when that hadn't been enough, turned him on by touching herself and sharing every filthy detail. She'd come shouting his name, and he hadn't lasted much longer.

He'd woken this morning with a stone in his gut.

Beau hadn't made his decision because of April, but without her, he'd never have known what it felt like to have something else. Something that wasn't *this*.

The reins had been tightening for years, and now the noose had settled too close. She was a lifeline, an escape, and a haven all in one.

And he was done holding back.

Rebecca shook her head. "Stop pacing or you'll wear your shoes out. By the way, I've sent your suit for the gala to your apartment, and I RSVP'd with a plus-one like you asked."

"Thank you." All of his clothes felt too tight. Maybe he should have waited until closer to the gala.

"You're making the right choice."

His smile dropped as soon as the door opened, JP's stormy face an ominous sign.

Rebecca said her good nights and left them. JP said nothing.

Love is for the brave.

Beau stood his ground. "You've heard."

"I have." JP hadn't moved from the doorway, keeping Beau trapped. It was an alarmingly effective tactic. "Let's ignore the fact that you didn't come to me first. Do you mind telling me why?"

He would *not* let his father intimidate him.

"You're going to want to sit down first."

JP remained silent, unmoving, as Beau did his best to explain.

"It's not what you wanted, but I've spent enough of my life —"

"Beau, stop."

He knew that tone. Had heard it his whole life.

When he'd practiced this speech, he'd imagined his father's reaction — displeasure creasing the corners of his eyes and mouth, and a weighted stare that straddled the intersection of cold and barren.

He hadn't expected to find defeat.

For the first time in his life, JP wasn't meeting *his* gaze. His head was bowed, eyes lowered to his lap. It was unnerving.

Even in this, JP had the upper hand. Beau couldn't help but be a little impressed.

"Ms. Nelson — Bonnie — is a fine choice, and I welcome her transition into the role. In fact, it is a choice I would have made myself if I hadn't wanted you to take my place."

With this, he looked up. "But," JP added, "I'm disappointed that you didn't discuss this with me earlier. Am I really that unreasonable?"

Yes.

Had JP never looked in a mirror?

"You've made it clear who I was supposed to be from the day I was born. And each time I veered off that path, you told me exactly how much of a disappointment I was. I knew you wouldn't approve of this."

"Well, you're wrong."

And.

Fuck.

Beau had expected the words, but… this whole scene was playing out of order. JP was supposed to yell and remind Beau that he was wasting his potential. Throwing away generations of their family legacy.

But instead, he sat there, his mouth turned down, looking for all the world like Beau had hurt his feelings.

JP wasn't supposed to *have* feelings.

His father sighed.

"If you're looking for an apology, I'm not sure I can give you one. I had my reasons, and when I see the man you've grown into, I see someone I'm proud of. I won't be sorry about that." He cleared his throat. "But I know I haven't been the easiest person to live with, and I wasn't the father you needed. For that I apologize. I don't know that I could have done it any differently. I love you, Beau, and I haven't said that enough. If leaving is what you want…" He stopped, taking a long, labored breath. "Then I support your decision. I only hope that you will stay in contact afterward. I've grown accustomed to seeing you."

Well, shit. Who knew JP could punch as hard emotionally as he just had? Beau was floored. Speechless.

"Is it too early for whiskey?" he said when he could trust his voice not to crack.

JP rose from his seat. "No."

His father walked over to the bureau and poured a single glass. Not two, just one.

When it was pressed into Beau's outstretched hand, the shock of the gesture choked him.

Beau downed the spirit in one shot. It burned and did nothing to distract from how completely bizarre this conversation had become, but the rising tide of emotion eased off, clearing Beau's lungs for a deep, steadying breath.

"Better?" JP asked.

Beau nodded. "I don't understand where this is coming from."

"Life becomes precious when so little of it remains. I don't want to waste the time we have left."

A part of Beau wanted to rage. They'd had years of time, decades, and one half apology didn't come close to fixing that, but he was right. They were running out.

Damn him for pulling that card.

Suddenly, JP was in front of him, refilling his glass.

"Your grandfather didn't enjoy music. Did you know that? Said he didn't understand it. And he certainly hated the idea of me becoming a musician."

Beau froze. JP... a musician? Had the world turned inside out?

A smile cracked through JP's stern features, an almost invisible quirk of the lips, but it was so genuine it blew through Beau with a force. It was the most candid he'd ever seen JP.

"I used to sneak out to blues clubs and dive bars. Anywhere that had an open mic, I'd be there, guitar in hand. George was furious. He talked to the owners, made sure they wouldn't let me play. Reminded me that the business was more important. And he was right, of course. Music was a distraction, and eventually, I stepped up, took my place at his side."

Beau counted his breaths as he listened. How had he never known this? His whole life, he'd thought of his father as a corporate wunderkind, a man truly born for politics.

That once upon a time, he'd simply been Jonathon, a young guy with a dream, was difficult to reconcile.

"Were you any good?"

Beau had never seen his father's eyes light up before. There'd been hints, he realized now, when they'd discussed music, and it hit him — the records, the conversations. All this time, JP had been reaching out, attempting to connect. Trying to share a piece of himself.

Beau blinked as his eyes went hot.

"I was, actually. Not sure how much of it I still have. The stroke took a lot of mobility from my fingers, but I can still strum a decent tune."

JP smiled. Actually, *genuinely* smiled, and *Christ*... it was hands down more impossible than his connection with April.

Beau was going to need a minute.

Luckily, his father was never lost for words. "You mentioned a young woman."

"April." He didn't hide his smile. "She's incredible. I'm going to marry her if she'll have me." And if she wanted to. Hell, if she wanted to have a symbolic ceremony under the stars of the new moon on the Easter equinox, he'd say yes.

If it meant being with her, he was there. Signed, sealed, delivered. For life.

"Tell me about her."

And so he did.

It was possibly the longest conversation they'd ever had, and easily the strangest. Maybe his declining health had softened his father, or maybe they were finally *hearing* each other, but JP kept asking questions and Beau kept answering them.

And the longer they talked, the stronger his need grew to come clean with April.

It was only fair. She knew the truth of him, but he had kept her from the facts.

It weighed on Beau, slipped its tendrils around his lungs, trapping every breath with the doubt that once she found out, she'd leave. Not only because he'd lied by omission, but because being a Forrester came with certain… expectations.

In the time they'd spent together, her kind heart and sour wit had slowly filled in the cracks of his heart. Despite the distance, she'd left indelible marks, and he never wanted to be without her. Without ever touching, she'd made him a new man.

———

He held the swans in his hands, stroking their delicate necks, before returning them to his nightstand, nestled beside a tattered Agatha Christie novel Rebecca had sourced for him. April had challenged him to guess the ending, even though he hadn't read anything for fun in a decade.

He hadn't guessed it but had kept the book anyway.

April already occupied his every thought, so it was natural to want a piece of her in his home. It looked good there. It fit.

"I want to meet you."

It was still relatively early in the evening, the sun winking over the horizon, squeezing between apartment blocks as shadows stretched out across the city. He tried not to take it as a bad sign.

He undid two buttons at his throat.

"Beau. I don't think that's a good idea."

"Why not? We have something here. You know we do."

Years of shadowing JP was no help to him here. Beau could navigate an international board meeting but had exactly zero experience with love. He was flying blind.

"I was resigned to a half-life before we met. Be brave with me."

"I want to… but…"

"Is it because I haven't told you my name? You can have it. It's Beau Aaron Forrester. Son of Jonathon, heir to the Forrester fortune, and soon to be demoted COO. I don't want to keep anything from you anymore. I want to give you everything."

Immediate silence. No breathiness, no laughter,

nothing. It lasted so long he could hear the couple downstairs shuffling around.

Definitely a bad sign.

"April?"

"I'm here."

His heart was pounding.

"Did you not want to know?" It was his greatest fear. After all this time, weeks of welcoming her into every corner of his heart, corrupted by his last name. His folly, yet again.

He'd hoped that she had seen past that. Seen the real him.

"That's not… I'm glad you told me."

This was all wrong. Her voice held none of its usual warmth. All of it — the short sentences, the hesitation — pressed harder against his chest. He slipped another button loose from his collar, lost the vest, rolled up his cuffs.

All the while, April was quiet.

He was so fucking done with silence.

"Meet me," he pleaded, pouring himself another whiskey. He would regret it come morning, but he'd deal with that later. Deal with it all later. "It doesn't have to mean anything," *Liar.* "We can take it slow, start with a chat or coffee. But… I'd like to see you in person. And if you meet me, and you want to end it…"

The thought was too painful to finish.

"Saturday at noon. I'll be waiting at the riverside café. Meet me there."

Still there was silence. Had he lost her?

"Please."

"I'll think about it."

———

Beau fought the urge to throw his glass to the floor, his whiskey turned to ash in his mouth. He'd ruined it. Asked too soon. Pushed too hard.

Been too emotional.

And the fucking problem couldn't be solved in any way available to him. Being a Forrester didn't mean a thing when it kept him from the woman he loved.

He'd been foolish to hope she'd see past all the bull-shit. That she'd know he was worth more than the money and the name.

That she could love him for him.

His longing, once familiar, comforting even, was suddenly smothering. A crushing weight pulling him deeper.

The loss of her voice, the warmth of her laugh, the teasing that had made him feel lighter, brighter — it left a gaping hole. He didn't even know what she looked like. Only what she'd told him. Only what he'd imagined.

There was no physical presence to miss, and yet he missed her in every part of his body. The gaps between his fingers, the crook of his arm, his chest, his cock.

He struggled to take a full breath. It still wasn't enough. *He* wasn't enough.

Chapter Twelve

April's birthday had always been a joyous occasion. She'd taken the opportunity to carefully guilt her brothers into making the trip in so that the whole family would be together.

They had never needed much growing up, and the years of living in each other's pockets under one roof were some of the happiest memories April had.

It wasn't strange to be choked up today. Except it had nothing to do with her family and everything to do with Beau.

Beau Aaron Forrester, officially. Arguably the most influential man in Chance, and the love of her life.

A last name shouldn't carry so much weight. But it wasn't the fan pages or high-profile ex-girlfriends or mind-blowing net worth that scared her.

Okay, the net worth was a little confronting, but everything she could find about Beau only reinforced what she already knew. Here was a man who cared about his city, used his status to champion philanthropic efforts, and rarely flaunted his wealth.

Here was a man whose reality overshadowed the fantasy in all the best ways.

Beau was real. Real… and *familiar*.

Her office neighbor, the one she'd waved to, worked alongside, smiled at, was Beau. They had caught the same train home.

How many times had she had the opportunity to talk to him and let it pass her by?

Beau had showed his hand, and now the move was April's. He still didn't know who she was. The ball was entirely in her court, and she was too scared to make a move.

April swallowed back the knot in her throat.

It was ridiculous to be upset, surely. She'd known this was coming, even though she had furiously hoped she'd have more time.

What the hell was she going to do?

————

Helena's in-progress creations were lined up on a shelf beside the window, the linen curtain fluttering gently above them, casting a kaleidoscope of patterns through the room. As a little girl, April had lain on the floor, tracing the patterns with markers, fascinated by the geometry. She hadn't inherited a single ounce of her mom's artistic talent, but at least she could share her space.

April traced the spine of a stem vase. It was time, she knew that. The impasse between her and Helena had been steadily growing since Eli had gotten married last year.

"I never knew what a fractal was until you were in school."

April turned to face her mom, who leaned against the door frame, her arms and legs crossed and her white hair glowing in the daylight. She looked like a painting.

"I used to have your dad quiz me after you'd gone to bed, but I've always been terrible at math, so none of it stuck. Honestly, you're lucky you take after him."

April smiled, her chest tight. Beau's voice rang through her ears. *You're not a coward.* "I'm sorry I've disappointed you."

Helena wrapped her in a hug before April could take her next breath. "What are you talking about? You could never disappoint me."

April clung to her. It had been so long since she'd been held, and it only made her miss Beau more. "I know you wanted me to be more like Ruby, with a husband and kids by now."

Pulling back, her mom framed her face with roughened hands. She smelled like earth and paint and *home*.

"I don't want you to be like Ruby. We couldn't possibly fit all that melodrama in one room." Her mouth flattened. "I don't want you to be anyone but yourself. I'm sorry that I've been pushing you. I see how happy your brothers and your sister are, and I want that for you too. You're so special April, and you deserve someone who will make you happy. But I'm also aware that that is very old-fashioned of me, and I never want you to think you need a partner to validate you."

Oh god, she was trying so hard… April was going to cry. Right here, on her birthday, surrounded by her mom's half-finished projects. Overcome, she ducked her head, resting against her mom's shoulder. "I know all of that…"

"I sense a *but* coming."

It was harder than April had expected. How did Beau make it all sound so easy?

"I know you gave up a gallery position when Dad lost his job, but I'm not like that. If I had to choose between work and love, I couldn't give up everything I've worked for. So it's better if I don't get anyone's hopes up."

"Oh honey. The right person wouldn't ask you to choose." Helena's arms tightened around her. "The day your father lost his job, I suspected I was pregnant with your brother. My old boss had been trying to convince me to take a permanent position for months. I called him and accepted as soon as I'd spoken to your dad. We then purposefully misremembered our conception date so that I was eligible for maternity leave."

April smiled as her mom pressed a kiss to her forehead.

"I never once regretted the decision. Having a family had always been a priority, so I did what was best for you kids. And *if*," she stressed the word, "you ever fall in love, it'll be with someone who supports your priorities, whatever they are. Or else they'll have to deal with me."

April stepped back, raising her hand to wipe at the tear clinging to her lashes. "I think maybe I am in love."

Helena lit up. "What? Who? And why didn't you tell me? I want to know everything."

"So, funny story…"

———

By the time April finished, the whole family was gathered around the dining table, scraping cake off their plates. Felix was curled up on Helena's lap, while Ruby and Liam were staring at an article about Beau they'd found online, their mouths wide. Beside her, Eli quietly explained their shock to their father.

She wasn't sure if she should be embarrassed or proud — they were ogling her boyfriend, after all.

"One question," Liam asked. "Why are you here with us? This guy is the 1 percent. You could be on a yacht."

Helena reached across the table to smack his arm.

He just laughed. "What? It's a valid question."

April sighed. "Look at him." She waved at Ruby's phone. "His net worth is the size of a small nation, and he's spent his whole life rubbing shoulders with beautiful elites. What could he possibly see in a data scientist who works too much? My vacuum broke last week because the roller was clogged with hair. There's no way this doesn't end in disaster."

The chorus of groans made her blush.

Liam scowled. "If he cares about any of that shit, then he's an asshole with too much money and no sense."

Her dad's hand landed on hers. "You can't always guess the ending beforehand. Sometimes you've got to let the mystery play out and hope for the best."

April looked around the table, a pang in her chest for the people in her life. She didn't know what she'd do without them. And the reminder that Beau had grown up without the support of a close family only made her ache for him grow.

They may never have met, but that didn't diminish what she knew to be true — underneath the name and the obligations, he was gentle and kind. Could tease and seduce, and she still flushed when she remembered the way he'd asked her to come for him.

"What are you so afraid of?"

April looked at her sister, who frequently stressed over being a good mother and barely had time for herself, and yet she knew Ruby wouldn't change a thing.

"Right now, I'm who he imagines me to be. As a dream, I can't disappoint him. But once I'm real, then…" She couldn't finish.

It would be lazy to blame Preston, as the first man who had made her feel unwanted. A janky piece of data that threw off the end result. The outlier.

Beau could call her beautiful and brave all he wanted, but what happened if they met and the chemistry was gone? What about when they had their first fight? Or when he realized that April's stress-related insomnia wouldn't simply *go away* — because she loved solving problems and sometimes that meant waking up at one a.m. to write down the solution.

The last two months had been wonderful, but it wasn't *real*.

Ruby scoffed. "If he's disappointed by the real you, then he doesn't deserve you, and we'll make his life miserable." She laughed when Helena clicked her tongue.

"You've never been afraid to be yourself, April. Don't start now."

It was all too much. Tears fell from her eyes. Love like this was unquantifiable. There was no rhyme or reason to it, no boundaries, no conditions. When she questioned everything else, her family was there, reassuring her.

It was a love Beau had never grown up with. A love he didn't believe he deserved. And yet, it hadn't stopped him from letting his guard down. Despite his own fears, he'd opened up to her, and she'd turned away.

"I'm going to meet him," she declared. She had to make it right. When he reached out, she wanted to be his safe place.

"Ask him if he can get us reservations at that new sushi place downtown," Eli asked.

Helena rolled her eyes. "Leave him alone. You never know," she reached over to grab April's hand, "he might be family someday."

Chapter Thirteen

April's steps faltered when Beau came into view. He looked amazing — casual in a sky-blue polo and jeans, hair hung soft and loose around his face. Soft, sexy, and so, so real.

She wiped her palms on her dress, heart fluttering like mad. This was it. The first official test. Months of conversations, and here he was in front of her. Waiting, hoping.

He was gorgeous. Exactly as she remembered and also a thousand times more handsome because he was *Beau*. The same man who had cooked for her and kept her company in the middle of the night.

Tall, slim, fit. Clean shaven. His dark, wavy hair was tucked behind his ears, begging for April to put her hands through it. An ass that had its own hashtag.

Those pants should be illegal, the way they hugged his thighs.

The walk toward him was a gut-wrenching blend of

exhilaration and fear. What if he didn't like her family? Or hogged the sheets at night? Maybe he had a thing for feet, or he was a terrible kisser. So much could go wrong, and yet she didn't stop.

She blinked, and his eyes — those gorgeous, unfathomable eyes — were staring into hers, sparkling over the most amazing smile, full and boyish and god, she'd never noticed how his top lip kind of disappeared when he did that, but now it was all she could think about.

Quickly, he closed the distance until he stood an arm's length away. She'd never wanted to touch someone so badly. By his sides, he flexed his fingers. Not just her, then.

"Hi, Beau. I'm April."

Recognition lit his eyes on fire — a crystallized blue that burned brightly. Gone was the careful blankness he had worn on the train, replaced by a smile so wide April's knees almost gave out.

"It's you," he breathed. "I'd hoped, but —"

She couldn't stop staring. "Me too."

Between them, Beau reached for her, then stopped, closing his hand into a fist mid-air before lowering it and huffing out a short laugh. "I really need to hug you right now. Is that crazy?"

It was April's turn to laugh. "If you don't, I will. But I might never let go."

"I'm surprisingly okay with that."

As he wrapped his arms around her waist, she melted against him, sliding her hands up his — damn, he really did work out — hard chest and around his neck.

"See?" he whispered against her lips. "Perfect."

———

For Beau, love in general was a nebulous concept. What was love to someone who had only ever imagined it? Wanted it with every breath for a lifetime but never received it until now?

So love at first sight was a concept he'd never considered, but if he had, he would have imagined it like this.

April was warm beneath his fingers, and he was greedy for it, starved for touch and for her. Finally able to confirm that she was real and as beautiful as she'd sounded — long legs and rounded cheeks, her skin sun soaked and her smile blinding.

He cataloged each feature, slotting them in against everything he knew her to be — funny, shy, incredibly sharp, and loving. Her wide eyes sparkled with flashes of gold, her hair like gasoline to his heart. She was radiant, bursting with color and life.

"Is now a good time to tell you I was right?" he asked, stroking her cheek with the back of his hand. "You're beautiful."

Finally, he got to see her blush in all its glory, feel the heat of it. He couldn't look away, wasn't sure he'd ever stop. Now that she was here — and *my god, she'd actually come*. He wasn't dreaming this — the possibilities were endless.

"Your hair is so soft," she said, running her fingers through the ends. His body burned at every point of contact.

This was what he had been searching for.

He couldn't stop touching her, holding her close, breathing her in. For all the talking they'd done, he was at a loss for words. The last thing he needed was to say the wrong thing now.

"I'm really happy you changed your mind."

Her smile widened. "My family helped. But we might need to avoid them for a little while because they're kind of obsessed with you right now."

"Like I said it before. As long as you're here, I don't need anyone else."

She beamed, and he couldn't wait any longer, finally kissing her. She responded immediately, pulling him closer, and his heart damn near stopped when she made the soft, satisfied sound he'd come to know so well.

He deepened the kiss as her lips parted, fueled with every desire he'd had since they met. How was this real? Even with her pulse skittering under his palm, the heat of her body burning through her dress... it was hard to believe they were finally together.

He tangled a hand in her hair, gripping her waist with the other. The tie of her dress teased him, and he wanted nothing more than to unwrap her, lay her down, and make her his.

He couldn't stop touching her.

Their mouths fit together perfectly, his tongue insistent as it met hers. It was so fitting for it to be April, and for April to be the woman from across the way. The one he'd watched with curiosity, who'd shone so brightly, even from a distance.

When tears pricked his eyes, he pulled back. Finally having her in his arms, concrete proof that he hadn't made her up washed over him so suddenly, he could barely breathe. Until all he could do was drop his face to her shoulder and hold her close. April cradled him there, stroking assurances into his skin.

Softly, he pulled back, brushing the hair away to kiss her neck. He remembered every whispered word they'd shared. The way she wanted to be touched. Loved. He dragged his nose along the sensitive dip behind her ear, reveling in the way she shivered.

"I like this," he said, tracing her lips with his thumb before leaning down to kiss her gently. The curve of her lip tasted so sweet under his tongue.

"I need to make a confession." He almost lost himself when she pulled her lower lip between her teeth. The only remedy was to kiss her again. "There's no way I can be casual about this. At all. We don't have to rush anything, but you need to know that you're it for me."

———

"Beau," April said, cupping his face in her palms. She would never grow tired of his face. "I wouldn't be here if I wanted casual. I'm here because I want you."

He kissed her. "Good. Because I'm completely in love with you."

She was speechless. Thank god he was holding her because she couldn't feel the ground beneath her feet. How did he make it all look so easy?

Be brave.

"I love you too."

The smile on Beau's face broke like the sun over the horizon, dazzling. It was impossible to look away. And now that it was there, she never wanted it gone.

"Oh," April said as he pulled a stray hair from his shoulder. The first date wasn't even over, and she was shedding all over him. Good *god*, that was embarrassing. "You should probably get used to that."

"Touching you? I don't know that I'll ever get used to that," he said, cupping her cheek so gently she wanted to cry. "I don't think I ever want to."

Do you promise?

"Do you want to…" she hedged. She hardly knew where to start. Talk. Kiss. Spend forever.

"Yes," he said earnestly.

"I didn't say anything," she said, laughing, surprised, although she knew she shouldn't be. She couldn't stop it. She was floating.

"Everything." He brought his other hand up to her face, kissing her slowly. "I want everything."

She looped her arms around his neck again, pressing kisses to his jaw. He let her take what she wanted, and wasn't that a rush? Having someone as powerful and confident and sexy as Beau move so easily under her hand.

Beau's breath skittered along her skin, his low hum

even more incredible in person. "Can I take you home? I want to kiss you in every room, fall asleep where you dreamed of me." She shivered when he added, "And I really want to watch you fall apart while you scream my name."

————

April's heart drummed a frantic beat. Every dirty promise Beau had made had been fulfilled, and she couldn't get enough. If her body hadn't given out sometime after the third orgasm, she wouldn't have stopped.

Sweat dampened her skin, cooling in the late afternoon air. She'd left the window open again and hoped desperately that her upstairs neighbor wasn't home. Otherwise, she'd definitely be avoiding eye contact with him for a while.

Beau kissed the corner of her mouth, her cheek, her eyelid. He teased and stroked her body, barely lifting his hands from her. Constantly touching.

His chest was exactly as comfortable as she imagined it would be.

She lifted her head. "You really demoted yourself?"

He nodded, then kissed her again. "Bonnie agreed I'll be better off heading up our community partnership program. I've already signed the paperwork for the first recipient. It's a little marketplace my girlfriend introduced me to. I don't know if you know it."

"You —" April sprang up, her hand on Beau's chest.

"You saved the markets? Beau, that's amazing. I can't wait to tell my mom." Then, "Girlfriend?"

"Yes."

Just like that. A statement. A declaration.

"Okay," she said, kissing him. "Have I told I love you?"

"I don't remember," he teased. "Maybe tell me again, just in case."

"I'll say it so often you'll get sick of it."

"I find that hard to believe," he said, his voice suffused with so much warmth April might never feel cold again.

"Stranger things have happened." Despite the humidity, she moved closer. How could she extract herself now that she knew how comfortably they fit?

Eventually, she'd have to. Monday she'd have work. Beau would continue to assist Bonnie's transition, and they'd have to leave their naked cocoon to venture back into the real world.

But then, April realized, the missing piece of the puzzle finally falling into place, they'd come home. Together.

Epilogue

ONE YEAR LATER

With all the extra time on his hands, Beau had taken to cooking every night. Most mornings too, especially if he and April had stayed up late the night before. It was addictive — the way her face lit up when he brought her breakfast in bed, and the little moans of pleasure while she ate, usually leading to round two.

Dinner was almost complete, the pot simmering on the stove awaiting the final ingredients. Once the carrots were added, it could be left to cook, and Beau could clean up and set the table before April came home.

He'd never fussed about where he ate when he'd lived alone, but there was something possessive about marking out her spot in their shared space. Standing back and seeing the physical reminder that she was here.

Not that there weren't reminders of that already. Since she'd moved in, his apartment had transformed. Filled first by her presence, then her heart. His walls were now covered with photos of their families, including his father.

He placed the lid on the pot, lowering the gas so it would give them time together before it was ready. Beau walked to the bedroom, throwing a quick glance at the time on his way.

Everything was on track.

He showered — fast yet thoroughly. The smell of April's shampoo lingered, and he couldn't help closing his eyes and taking a deep breath. It spoke of mornings and nights spent in bed, the curl around his fingers as pressed her against the fridge, brushing it out of her eyes in the shower, kissing her temple while they walked the markets arm in arm.

He was throwing on a shirt when he heard her.

The telltale jingle of keys rang into the bedroom, followed quickly by the skittering of paws toward the front door. Her voice carried easily. "Yes, Milo, I'm happy to see you too. Okay, okay, let me get through the door first."

Beau chuckled to himself. Barely six months old, and Milo could hardly bear to tear himself away from April anytime she was home.

Like father, like pup.

A minute later, while Beau ran his hands through his

hair, the music changed, and he returned to the kitchen to find her eyeing the pot.

"Smells good," she said, her arms slipping around his shoulders.

"You smell better," he countered before sliding their lips together. It was slow and sweet, the gentle undoing of the day's stress as he mapped out her mouth with his.

"How are you feeling?" April asked, staying close.

Beau swallowed. JP had been gone now for three months. His grief, like everything with JP, was complicated.

"Better now that you're home." He reached out, brushed the silky red strands aside. "How did the workshop go?"

She sagged against him, her nose cold against his throat. "Good, but I'm glad it's over. They were happy with the trends we spotted, so now I have a series of reports to build so we can monitor the next month and mmm —"

He nipped at her soft lips before deepening the kiss. She tasted like the terrible office coffee she'd drunk, probably her fifth for the day, and Beau didn't care. He couldn't get enough of her.

"Christ, you're sexy when you're brilliant."

Her moans always tasted so sweet.

"Tell me again," she whispered.

Beau nibbled on her ear, smiling against the sensitive skin along her neck as she shivered and bucked against him. "I love you."

She fit so perfectly against him, a fresh reminder of

how she'd woken him this morning, with her hands and her mouth and her devotion, surrounding him in heat and love.

Then, with the sharp note of a trumpet ringing through the apartment, he pulled away.

"Is this?"

"Happy birthday, Beau."

He could hardly believe it, but, yep, this was the rare live performance every Davis fan prayed they could get their hands on. Even JP had coveted it, with no luck.

"How?"

Her hands found their way to his hair, sensation curling around his spine and straight to his cock as she worked her fingers through the strands.

"I had no idea robotics engineers were such nerds about jazz, but I pulled in a favor."

"You're incredible." He picked her up, arms tight around the waist, and twirled her. "Marry me."

"I can't, we're already engaged," she laughed.

"I don't see why that matters," he found her mouth again. And again, and again. "Shit, that blows my present out of the water." He'd almost forgotten.

"Beau, it's your birthday. You shouldn't have gotten me anything."

"I like spoiling you. What's wrong with that? Besides, you said you liked the view." He held out a set of keys, and her eyes widened.

"Oh Beau, did you really? Over the park?"

"The very same. This way you'll be closer to work but still within walking distance from your parents."

April launched herself at him, and he caught her, settling her thighs around him and grinding against her while she moaned.

"What about dinner?" she asked, already breathless.

He sucked a series of kisses along her collarbone, drinking in her moans. "It needs to simmer for forty minutes, so we have some time to kill."

"Couch?"

He shook his head, planting her on the dining table. She spread her legs, and he slid his hands up her thighs, hooking his fingers under her underwear and pulling them off.

With a hand on her shoulder, he coaxed her to lie down. Her breasts rose and fell heavily with each panted breath. The inside of her thighs glistened. "You're gorgeous."

Even after a year of dating and fucking and living together, she blushed so prettily when he complimented her.

Beau dropped to his knees. Dinner needed another forty minutes, and he wasn't going to waste a single second of it.

THE END

Thank you!

I can't thank you enough for reading A Missing Connection! I hope you enjoyed reading it as much as I enjoyed writing it.

Want to share the love? Please consider leaving a review on Amazon, Goodreads, or even posting wherever you hang out online (BookTok, Bookstagram, Reddit). Comments and tags feed my romance reading soul.

I absolutely love to hear from my readers.

Dani x

Acknowledgments

Firstly, as always the biggest shout outs to Sam from Ink and Laurel for the most incredible cover and Beth Lawson my editor, you astound me every time.

A huge thank you to Nellie Wilson for beta reading and loving Beau (and THAT scene) as much as I do. Your friendship means the absolute world to me.

To the wonderful writers who inspire me — I am so lucky to call you friend. The fact you respond to my messages continues to surprise me. You're all amazing women and every time I read your work I am reminded what is possible and how powerful stories can be when you allow yourself to be vulnerable.

To every reader who gave this book a chance, my gratitude is immense. To every reader who shares their favorite parts with me, thank you for always reminding me why I love doing what I do.

Thank you to my family and friends for your forever support. It still hasn't quite sunk in that this is a job I get to do, and you have never stopped reminding me to be proud of myself.

About the Author

Dani McLean is an emerging author of Contemporary Romance stories that feature kickass women who can't quite get their shit together, and the irresistible but confused men who fall in love with them.

Born in Melbourne, she now lives in Perth, Western Australia with two walk in robes and a linen closet that's full of wine.

Dani loves to read, write and travel (in her memories, these days). She loves Hallmark movies because they're unintentionally hilarious, she's been on enough terrible Tinder dates to fuel countless books; and when she isn't conducting unofficial wine tastings in her pyjamas, she's devouring all things romance.

instagram.com/dmc_lean

facebook.com/danimcleanfiction

twitter.com/dmc_lean

tiktok.com/dmc_lean

amazon.com/author/danimclean

goodreads.com/danimclean

bookbub.com/authors/dani-mclean

CPSIA information can be obtained
at www.ICGtesting.com
Printed in the USA
BVHW032322140223
658501BV00004B/115

9 780645 533347